The Night Sweeps the Mountains Away

THE NIGHT SWEEPS THE MOUNTAINS AWAY

TANVIR AHMED

Dancing Star
Press

This is a work of fiction. Names, characters, organizations, events, and incidents are either products of the author's imagination or are used fictitiously.

All translations from Pashto, Persian, and Arabic by Tanvir Ahmed

Copyright © 2026 Tanvir Ahmed

All rights reserved.

No part of this book may be used or reproduced in any manner for the purpose of training artificial intelligence technologies or systems.

The Night Sweeps the Mountains Away by Tanvir Ahmed

First published by Dancing Star Press 2026

www.dancingstarpress.com

Cover illustration by Guoldu

ISBN: 978-1-7321418-8-9 (paperback) 978-1-7321418-9-6 (ebook)

10 9 8 7 6 5 4 3 2 1

For Caro

جان می‌دمد از لعلت چون برق اگر خندد

بیدل

اوبه په دانګ نه بیلیږی

ناشناس

Chapter One

تیر شه درست عمر ثما په دا هوس

که می وپوبنتي چه څوک ئی یا څه کس

رحمان

The first time I met Mina, I saw the story written at the corner of her eye. A diamond in four dots, nested between her right temple and the edge of her eyebrow. To most it would look like a beauty mark. I knew better.

I met her toward summer's end, as the winds began to settle and the markets swelled with the year's last eastbound caravans. At the time, I was making a living as a water carrier. I spent most days loping between the public wells and my clients' houses, waiting with the women and nomads to fill my leather bag, hauling it through the dust and clamor of the streets, forcing a smile as doors opened for me. I made enough for my daily bread, and did not have to ask for alms.

I had several clients in the area of the Gulistan Gate, a quiet neighborhood shaded by fragrant olive trees. The air there was sweetened by birdsong and scents from unseen gardens. I was near to an invisible presence myself, part of the neighborhood's heartbeat, no different from its sparrows or strays. No one asked who my people were, where I was from, what my story was. It was better that way, I would tell myself: to be forgotten, and to forget.

But that summer there were many questions about the neighborhood's newest resident. She had moved in shortly after the nomads began passing through town with their sheep and horses, as they did every year. The woman kept to herself and seemed to live alone. She never answered her door during the day. Some said they heard singing from her house after dusk. Few could claim to have actually seen her. I overheard more than one client guessing who she was. A merchant's wife whose husband was abroad. A rich man's daughter living off an inheritance. A runaway bride. A prostitute.

For my part the gossip left me curious, but I did not share my clients' fears about the neighborhood's reputation, or the example being set for their children. The woman wanted to be left alone. I could sympathize with the desire to avoid attention. Nonetheless, I decided to call upon her and offer my services. My livelihood was built on clients, and even recluses needed water.

I met her on a Thursday evening, not long after the call for sunset prayer. Shadows pooled on the lanes, and the sky was coppered by the last light of day. The thrushes had gathered for a late conference in the neighborhood's boughs. Part of me did not expect an answer when I knocked on the woman's door. I was surprised when it opened.

She was tall and thin, and stared back at me with eyes large and dark as a deer's. The skin under them was bruised by poor sleep. Her silk shawl had once been fine, stitched with subtle but faded embroidery. She had a common tattoo below her lower lip, a diamond in four dots. But it was her other tattoo, the same shape at the corner of her right eye, that left my mouth dry.

I stumbled through an introduction, all the while trying not to stare at that second tattoo. If she noticed my shock, she gave no sign of it. She considered me after I finished speaking, then told me to come back the following evening.

That night I could not sleep. The tattoo was a coincidence, I told myself, or a trick of the gloom, or something I had dreamed at the end of a tiring day. I had not seen its like in six years. The only women left with such a mark lived far from this desert town. They had tattooed their eyes just before the end of Sher Khan's rebellion, when there was no hope of victory left. Sher Khan's body had been scattered not long after that, and his people with it. Better to forget.

The next evening I called on the woman, and she led me into her courtyard. The balconies had been built to keep the sunlight from striking the ground. At the heart of the courtyard was a cistern, a few bright tiles clinging to its bricks. I unslung my bag and started to pour.

The woman waited by the door. When I finished, she handed me a mohur, which was far too much. I lifted my gaze to protest. Once again I saw the tattoo by her eye, unmistakable even in the deepening dusk, and it was as if a falcon had flown off with my spirit.

I began to pass by her home every few evenings. Each time, I told myself that the mark by her eye did not matter. There was no bringing Sher Khan back from the grave. Even if the woman had once claimed his people as her own, she and I were nothing to one another now. She owned a house while I filled its reserves. Perhaps she too was trying to forget.

I resolved to say nothing and leave it be. Yet every so often I found myself glancing at her face, longing for a glimpse of that tattoo.

Days passed before things shifted between us. I had just been paid, the gold heavy in my hand. The two of us were standing at the courtyard door. The sun had fallen away, the dark was blossoming. My eyes lingered a little too long.

"Where are you from?" she said, without preamble.

I was startled by her directness. The only safe course was to make something up and never set foot in her house again. I had hardly spoken the truth to another creature for six years.

"Giri," I said, before I could think better of it.

The woman looked at me, and I could not read her expression. Then she said, "I'm from Aghazpur."

Something long snarled in the hollows of my chest loosened. "I know the name." Of course I knew the name. What the King's soldiers had done at Aghazpur could hardly be forgotten.

"I thought you might," she replied.

"How did you know?"

"I suspected. I saw you recognize my tattoo."

"Any one of the King's soldiers might have recognized it too."

"They wouldn't look at me the way you do." The woman glanced at my bag. "Have you been here long?"

"Since the end, almost," I replied.

There was a fresh shadow of interest on her voice. "You never went to the highlands?"

"I was in prison when they resettled most of us."

"Do you ever wish you had gone?"

My gaze went to the tattoo by her eye again. "Often enough."

"Yet here you are."

"So are you."

The corner of her mouth twitched. Or perhaps it was a trick of the fading light.

For a time, our exchanges remained brief and banal. We spoke of the shifting season, of news overheard at the hammam or market. Some days we only spoke in greeting and farewell. I did not ask her name and she did not give it. Not once did we mention the old country, Sher Khan, the rebellion, the resettlement. I felt pulled to her even so, the force of it strong and strange, like that which called pigeons to their roosts, or drew the wandering stars along their paths.

Our evenings were not without risk. There has always been an evil reputation attached to men like me, porters and gardeners and others who enter houses while the men who own them are absent. The residents of the Gulistan Gate were already suspicious of their newest neighbor. People might talk. It was the sort of thing that could cost me clients, even attract the kotwal's attention. Neither she nor I could afford an arrest, for the remains of our people were under royal mandate to live only where we had been sent.

Still I would go to her door, and she always opened it for me.

About two weeks after we first spoke, after I filled the cistern, she asked if I wanted tea. I followed her into a mehmankhana spread with a beautiful kilim, blue birds in flight across a heaven woven from crimson silk. Bowls of orange blossoms stood in the corners, charpoys pressed between them.

I eased myself down onto one while the woman lit a samovar. She removed her shawl and set it aside. Her robe was black, her hair unbound, and I wondered if she was a widow. When she handed me a cup, I caught an iron tang from her hand.

The woman sat across from me, her own cup untouched by her foot. I took a sip. The tea was terrible, bitter from too long a steeping. I kept a straight face.

"I would offer you something to eat, but there's not much here," she said.

"I'm not hungry," I said. "But I can go bring something for you. Some of the stalls by the Friday Mosque stay open until the night prayers end."

"I will go out later," she said.

Not many women from the neighborhood did so after dusk, but I did not voice the thought. "You have a beautiful home," I said instead.

"It's yours when I leave."

I stopped with my cup raised halfway. "What do you mean?"

"I never stay in one place for long." She paused. "People start to talk."

I thought of the rumors, of how the truth of her was more dangerous still. "You're leaving the neighborhood?"

"I'm leaving town."

I struggled to keep the surprise from my face. "Where will you go?"

She pursed her lips. "Elsewhere."

Her word opened an unseen wound. I had no right to feel hurt, of course. Even so, her presence had shifted the pattern of my days. The recognition between us was a nourishing rain, letting some seed buried long ago sprout up through my ribs once more. I could not imagine how it might keep growing without her. I wanted her to reconsider, and had no idea how to ask.

"If this is about the gossip..." I started to say.

"It's more than that." She seemed about to continue, but did not.

I pressed the matter. "If you need help, all you have to do is ask."

She tilted her head and I could have sworn her eyes gleamed amber. "You don't know my situation."

"I know who you are," I replied. "That is enough."

"After everything, you still believe that?"

I said nothing.

The woman looked out to the courtyard. The night was unfurling outside though the lamplight held it at bay. Her hair curled across the side of her face, obscuring the tattoo at her eye.

"I was eighteen years old when Sher Khan was killed," she said, still gazing at the night. The breeze was sweeping some of the heat from the air. From beyond the courtyard, I could hear the rustle and swoosh of branches, heavy with the last blooming of the year. The woman's voice was measured as she began her tale.

The Woman from Gulistan Gate

I was eighteen years old when Sher Khan was killed. I never saw him, had nothing to do with him at the start. Of course I despised the soldiers who came to take our young men for the corvee, same as everyone else, but not enough to rise up and kill them: though I never had a brother worked to death building some governor's mansion, or a husband killed in a foreign war not his own. But I was at Aghaz-pur when the King's army came for revenge, and even if I hadn't come to Sher Khan's banner early, I went under its shade after that.

I heard that they had killed him when the King's men rode into our encampment. They jeered news of his dismemberment at us during the roundup, told us again and again in the stockade how his body had been scattered. When I heard we were to be exiled to the highlands, I was almost grateful.

My branch of our people ended up in one of the furthest valleys. It was hard, and not only because the country was not our own. It belonged to others who were already there, and they were not happy to see us. They had named the valley in their language after the ancient castle of honeycombed stone overlooking it. We started calling the valley after the same ruin, but in our own tongue, saying Dara Qala.

The King resettled us in the autumn, well into the second harvest, so there was no time to grow anything. Some of our people went to the governor and asked him to open his storehouses. Others refused to eat from the same hand that had beaten us and turned to raiding instead. A few went down to waylay merchants on the trade roads, and a few turned their eyes to our new neighbors' farms. They asked my uncle to join them, but even burdened as he was by caring for the remains of our family, he refused. He thought it went against our dignity. He went to our mullah instead, asking him to mediate between our people and the locals. The mullah replied the locals were pagans, descended from foreign barbarian soldiers, and that all they owned belonged to believers by holy law. I guess he forgot that he too had been someone else's barbarian not that long ago.

The next few years were no better. Our people started splitting apart like a rotten tree. The best fed were those who had made an arrangement with the governor, sending young men to his fields and levies in exchange for grain. Some of us tried trading with the locals, but they were as poor as we were, and would have nothing to do with us after the raids. My uncle wanted me to marry one of their boys to make peace if he would convert. They refused the proposal. I can't say I blame them.

Then the dervish came.

It was the edge of autumn. I had turned twenty, and even my mule of an uncle was contemplating a trip to the governor's tower. I was working at the home of Bibi Sayeda, whose embroidery was fine enough to fetch good prices in the lowland melas and bazaars. I cooked and cleaned and helped with her craft and she would send me home with enough to keep my family from going hungry.

One night I came home to find my uncle sitting with my cousins around the samovar, face flushed, eyes glinting. He had not even taken off his traveling robe, it was still stained from the road. I listened from behind the next room's curtain while putting out leftovers.

"A holy man has come," my uncle was saying. "Some of the merchants ran into him at sunset in the wood. Even before he came into sight they heard him singing in some foreign tongue. They say he is a great tall fellow with his head shaved into patterns. A real dervish."

My aunt was quiet. She respected the saints, more than her husband even, but was more cautious by nature. "What would a dervish be doing all the way up here?"

"Who knows the hearts of God's friends but God?" my uncle replied. "The merchants say that when they went to kiss his hand he spoke with an unknown accent. He's come from a distant land. Persia maybe, or even the kingdom of the Turks."

"What did he say?" my aunt asked.

My uncle spoke with the awe he usually reserved for the Quran. "He said soon the poor would inherit the world, the hungry would soon be satisfied, the weepers would soon be laughing, and the gluttons will soon be starving."

"But what does that mean?" my aunt said.

"We must welcome him," my uncle said. "If we seek the dervish's blessing, perhaps our fate will change. Even after Taimur, the Lord of the Auspicious Conjunction, conquered the seven climes, he would kiss the feet of the fakirs before issuing his decrees."

"Perhaps," my aunt said.

It was not long before news of the dervish began to spread in Dara Qala. A carpenter glimpsed him leading a pair of shaggy camels through the woods. How such great beasts had made their way up into the highlands was unclear. Traders heard disembodied singing in the hills at nighttime. Once, a band of woodsmen returned shaken, saying that a foul wind had knocked them off their feet at dusk. When they got back up, they briefly saw a tall and mysterious figure among them.

One morning, a shepherd came hurrying down the cattle track with news. The dervish had settled in the castle above the vale.

Before the sun could climb to its zenith, our leading men came together and set off to meet the mysterious holy man. My uncle was among them. His eyes were sparking with hope as he left.

Bibi Sayeda was more skeptical. "People should be careful," she said, setting aside an unfinished robe to take the meal I had prepared, fried bread folded around scallions. "We don't know that this stranger is a real holy man. You wouldn't let a fake physician tend your body, you shouldn't let a fake dervish tend your soul."

"We could use a blessing, though," I ventured. Bibi Sayeda daunted me. With her lips like tulip petals and eyebrows bent like ready bows, she was the most gorgeous person in the valley. Despite her fine needlework, she tended to dress carelessly. Time and the rebellion had left her hair silver and her frame frail, but her mind and tongue were sharp as always.

"Do you think Sher Khan sat around waiting for a holy man's blessing?" Bibi Sayeda said.

"Some are saying that's the reason we lost the war. That Sher Khan should have sought the permission of the friends of God before rising up."

Bibi Sayeda scowled. "Let anyone who says so get eaten by black bullets. Sher Khan was more a friend of God than any naked dervish rattling his bowl for alms from people who are already hungry. At least he picked up a sword and got brave, instead of sucking the heart's blood from the poor."

"We need hope," I said, parroting my uncle. "Our fate has to change."

"So let us change it ourselves. We stood up against evil once, we can do it again."

"You cannot be serious."

"Of course I am serious. This land is good ground, much higher and better than our own country for a fight. And the locals do not love the King any more than we do."

"We lost the last fight. We're even worse off now than we were then."

"We don't have to be." Bibi Sayeda took my hand and pinned me with a stare. The tattoo at the corner of her eye was stark against her skin. "Listen, Mina. You want to change your fortune, you do it with your own hands. Never put yourself into the hands of another."

But even Bibi Sayeda was curious after the headmen came back down from the castle. The men crowded into the common hujra to hear their report. I went with Bibi Sayeda to stand at the outside wall with some other women, listening in.

The headmen had come upon the dervish in the ancient castle's darbar, where he had been humming to himself. There they had placed an offering fresh from the harvest at the dervish's feet. Instead of accepting it, the dervish had commanded them to name their enemy. Most of the men were taken aback, did not know what to say. It was not the sort of thing a dervish would ask. But my uncle saw his chance and spoke into the quiet, naming the governor. The dervish rose up then and announced that divine judgment would befall this tyrant, and that through that punishment, the people would know his own power.

The news came a week later. One morning the governor's retainers had found him dead, throat torn out. It seemed as if some wild beast had done it. But how such an animal had passed in and out of the governor's high and fortified tower, none could say.

A stream of people began flowing to the castle after that. Some simply sought the dervish's blessing, touching his hand and kissing his feet. Others asked him to solve disputes or advise them about the future. Gifts began to brighten the ruin: new hangings for the pitted rooms, doors of fresh wood fitted to the arches, young trees for the courtyard, climbers for its crumbling walls. The dervish never gave his name, so we gave him one instead, calling him after his new haunt. He became our Dara Qala Sahib.

Even by the standards of dervishes, Dara Qala Sahib was peculiar. Many sainted beggars live off charity, but he refused all offerings of food or drink. He vanished for days at a time, reappearing without any rhyme or reason. He avoided the company of women and would not admit them into his presence. Some said, if quietly, that he could only speak to them in Persian and did so strangely, each word parted too cleanly from the rest.

Our people were not the only ones to seek the blessings of Dara Qala Sahib. The locals began visiting him with their own questions and complaints and wishes. Dara Qala Sahib took their hands as he had accepted ours. In his company, our two peoples at last sat knee to knee. And just as Bibi Sayeda had predicted, sitting together brought to light a common foe.

Taxmen's bodies showed up on the roads with their heads twisted wholly round. News came of the King's soldiers too, entire patrols discovered torn apart by wolves that left no traces and could not be found. When the mullah kept preaching that our unbelieving neighbors were not to be trusted and Dara Qala Sahib neither, we found his body tangled in the high boughs of a cedar tree.

The bad fortune of our enemies was mixed with a run of good luck for us. People who visited Dara Qala Sahib in the evenings sometimes woke to gifts in their courtyards: damasked bangles, pearl earrings, even some true gold. Men and women hurried off with them to the lowlands, and their mules returned laden with precious viands.

Of course, not all were enchanted by the miracles. The families who had prospered in the governor's service found themselves faring poorly. And some bigots could not stomach sitting down with the locals. Whispers turned to talk and talk turned to plans. One night, a band gathered in the blacksmith's house and set off for the castle. The sun rose on their corpses, strewn across Dara Qala's walls.

By then it was obvious Dara Qala Sahib was not only a holy man, but one of rare power. Some people began wondering if he was the prophesied Mahdi, come to fill the earth with justice before the end of days. My uncle was one of them. In that belief, even Sher Khan's death and the exile and our people's suffering became fair prices to pay for the blessing of Dara Qala Sahib. He walked proudly now, unafraid of hunger, rivals, tyrants. When Dara Qala Sahib announced his decision to take a bride, my uncle knew whom to offer.

The evening before I was set to marry Dara Qala Sahib, Bibi Sayeda gave me a handful of rupiyas and told me to run. She took my wrist with one hand and pressed the coins into my palm. Sometimes I can still smell the musk on her skin.

"I thought you said we should fight," I said.

Bibi Sayeda's expression was dark. "This is not fighting, Mina Jani. It's giving up."

"You still don't believe in him?"

Bibi Sayeda let my hand go, brushing her fingertips across the corner of my eye, across the tattoo that was a mirror to her own. "I believe in this."

"Sher Khan is dead."

"I am not talking about Sher Khan. I am talking about you, and every other woman who put the needles to her skin that night. Knowing we were going to lose, knowing we could not run, knowing we were marking ourselves as traitors for the rest of our lives. Knowing it all and doing it anyway."

I could feel a wind gathering in the hollows of my chest, a stirring panic I had to force down. "It does not matter anymore."

"It is all that matters," Bibi Sayeda said. "Mina, do not do this."

But I did it. I could tell you it was because I feared what would happen to our people if I angered one of the saints. I could say I did it because I did not know what else I could do, where I could go. I could say I did it because part of me believed in Dara Qala Sahib, or wanted to believe. All of it would be true.

It snowed the night before my wedding, though I had been too anxious to notice. The procession marched me through a bleached and washed out world beneath gray heavens, right up to the castle gate. There was a talisman on my forearm, a folded paper tied there with green thread, upon which Bibi Sayeda had scrawled the Throne Verse. I touched it over and over again as we made our way forward. I could feel the steep march up into the small of my back. My eyes were open but still full of bad dreams.

A handful of men met us at the castle's gate. These were Dara Qala's mystics, those who had left the world behind to dwell in the ruin with the dervish, clad now in patched wool, heads shaved in rough imitation of their master. My uncle was not one of them, though he too had scraped his pate bare. When he handed me over to the mystics, his pride was like sunlight splitting through the clouds above.

The mystics took me into the castle's darbar. The stone of the hall was scored all over, the roof had been thatched anew. The air was thick and musty. There were no other women.

At the end of the darbar, lounging across a dais draped with colorful quilts, was Dara Qala Sahib himself. His head was shaved into mandala patterns, just as they had said, but in place of a mendicant's wrap, he wore a striped silk robe. He seemed less like a friend of God than a man who would be king.

Someone took my arm and pulled me forward. I was all but swallowed up by the sight of my bridegroom. I shook with each step. As we drew close, Dara Qala Sahib rose at last, looming a full head over me, the breadth of him filling my vision. The air about him had the whiff of a battlefield. I could not say if he was my age or twice that or thrice.

There was no mullah to give the rites, no one who spoke to me at all. The officiant was Dara Qala Sahib himself. The whole process took place in a language I did not know, but the mystics punctuated the pauses with murmurs of ameen. I thought it must be Arabic even though none of the words sounded like the ones I recited in prayer.

Dara Qala Sahib finished speaking and my heart begged God to make the earth open up and swallow me whole. It was not because I had any foresight about what was about to happen to me. It was because in that moment, I truly saw him for the first time, so tall and strong and strange: and there I was, so completely alone.

Chapter Two

په سرپوبن محل کښې نور د آفتاب نوی

ښه دی زړه په یوه غم سره چاک چاک

حمید

Mina did not finish her account. The call for night prayer broke into her telling, leaving us too aware of both the hour and of ourselves. She noted the time and I got to my feet, still thinking about all that she had related. At her door, I turned and asked if she needed anything. She only said that she would see me on the morrow.

The next day was a Friday. After the noon prayer, I made my way to the Khan Bazaar. The market was a riot of mud-brick and pitted stone, its storefronts bright with copperware, leatherwork, and kilims. Some of the nomads had set up around the crossroads, hawking fleeces and bright robes and their most elegant ironwork. People were about in force, some for necessities, most simply to browse. Above us all rose the ramparts of the governor's palace.

I turned down one of the Khan Bazaar's branching alleys, coming to a cafe burrowed into the side of an old mansion. The walls were unpainted, the charpoys sagging. But the alley was quiet enough, the lattices opened onto a lush courtyard, and the fritters served with the coffee were generously sugared.

Qurban Ali was in our usual corner near the back, already sipping from a chipped cup. He wore a dun cap and a fringed shawl, and the sunlight clung to his neat beard. Leaning against the wall next to him was his rabab, his usual method for paying for a meal. He got up to greet me and tilted his head at something he saw.

"Is everything all right?" he said.

I assured him I was fine. We sat again and the owner brought me a cup. Soon enough, Qurban Ali was in the middle of a story about an awkward encounter with a mullah who fancied himself a poet and kept presenting him with fresh verses. Apparently the mullah was a gentle spirit and had a true passion, able to quote the lines of Saeb almost as well as the Quran. His criticisms were fresh and his insight novel. But the man could not compose two decent lines to save his life. Qurban Ali did not have the heart to tell him, but neither did he want to risk his own reputation by putting the mullah's poetry to song.

I did my best to pay attention, but my mind was wandering like a spurned lover. For years, I had done all I could to avoid thinking about Sher Khan's rebellion. The last time I had seen my own people was in prison. My time there was a patchwork of lightless cells, of forty bodies crammed into rooms meant for four, of a brutally wide courtyard hammered by the sun. I had languished there for weeks before soldiers came to take the survivors into the highlands. On the second night of the journey, I had slipped free.

Six years was a long time. Grief cauterized the heart, new sorrows came to wash away the old ones. Some days it seemed that all of it — Sher Khan, the uprising, the promise of the world it might bring — had been a hazy dream, the kind seen through eyes half open in the deep of night. Something which had at once been and not been. Then I had knocked on Mina's door and she had opened it, and I could no longer say whether I was dreaming or awake.

"Where have you gone, Sado?" Qurban Ali said.

His voice drew me back to the moment. I realized I had not been paying attention for some time. "I'm sorry," I said, embarrassed.

But there was no judgment in Qurban Ali's face. "I knew something was wrong the moment you walked in. There is a new weight to your step."

I looked at him. Qurban Ali was the only one who knew who I was and the past from which I had come. I had told him years ago, after a springtime mushaira held in the nearby orchards. That night, after the recitations ended and the rest of the poets were enjoying a meal, we had gotten a little tipsy. He had told me of his home country, the man there whom he had loved, his imprisonment, his flight. I had watched him as he spoke, seen the pain crackling behind his careful expression. Recognized in him another who could not speak of himself. So I had told him my own truths and trusted him to understand. I would have trusted him with this story, too, but it was not my story to tell.

"An old weight, not a new one," I finally said. "I was thinking of the past."

Qurban Ali smiled. "Not always a bad thing."

"Nothing can come of it."

"A shadowed tree will not bear fruit until brought to face the sun," Qurban Ali recited.

"I do not want fruit from this tree."

"Is that really the case, Sado Jana?"

I gave him a look, but did not reply.

"The tree will be there whether you want it or not," Qurban Ali said. "Give it light, chop it down, set it on fire, whatever you wish, but there is no use ignoring it."

"I have no idea what you are saying."

"Yes you do."

I sighed. "So what did you do with your tree?"

"Ah, Sado Jana," he said, smiling again, "I planted a whole orchard from it."

"This is why everyone finds singers irritating."

"Yet the finest people are always at our heels," he said. "Roshana Begum just sent me an invitation for her mushaira. You should come."

"Yes, bringing a stray day worker along to a poetry recital hosted by one of the wealthiest silk merchants around will certainly help you find more patrons."

"If people are offended, we'll just tell them the truth about who you are. It is romantic enough for patrons of poetry."

I only glared at him.

We took our time with the coffee, and Qurban Ali pushed me about the mushaira until I agreed to go. The conversation moved to a spate of recent animal attacks: a merchant found dead among the taverns, the corpses of two drunks turning up in an alley, a night watchman slain on patrol. All had been found with their throats savaged. It was thought the work of a dog or maybe a pack, likely escaped from a cruel family. Only the dogs of humans grew so feral.

Not until the call for afternoon prayer did I get up. Qurban Ali stayed behind, settling onto the floor and bending over his rabab. Soon he had fallen into a tune just shy of mournful, fingers soft on the strings. I lingered a while before going. I had some rare time to myself. There were no clients on Friday afternoons, save the one.

There was some time before I needed to be at her door, and I spent it on the move. I left the Khan Bazaar's bustle for calmer districts, making my way toward the edge of town. The poplars there pushed their way between shops and homes, throwing shade wide across the dust. People claimed the greenery was the remnant of some foreign prince's efforts to build a palace there. They said the trees had rebelled, digging their roots into foundation stones, stretching their branches through windows, hosting an army of birds to harry the workers.

I appreciated the trees for that story. But for my part, it was the neighborhood's stray dogs who had my affection. Strays recognize their own.

There was one in particular, a rangy gazelle hound with a matted gray coat, who often kept me company. I called him Khosh Qadam. Passing the humble shrine near his den, I spotted him padding out of an alley. He had long legs and a thin frame, and always seemed like he had been on the wrong end of a fight. Maybe that was why I liked him.

I never let Khosh Qadam follow me on my rounds. Some of my clients thought dogs unclean, and would never again let me near their water if they saw one at my side. But that Friday I had no one to see but Mina, and found myself wanting the company until then.

I bought an okra fry from a stall by the Friday Mosque, throwing pieces of the bread around it to Khosh Qadam. He followed me as I filled up my bag at the nearby well. A few women were there doing the same. Khosh Qadam lolled his tongue and panted happily at them. They edged away. The sky was darkening a shade too swiftly and the air was restless. There was a bad wind coming over the hills, though we were past the season for it.

Only when we reached Mina's door did I try to drive Khosh Qadam away. I used my most severe tone, urging him repeatedly to make himself scarce. Khosh Qadam did not budge, looking at me expectantly. I began to regret my impulse.

Mina opened the door though I had not knocked. Likely she had heard my fruitless efforts with Khosh Qadam. "I'm sorry," I said. "He is not very good at taking orders."

Mina considered Khosh Qadam. He took a cautious step forward, sniffing the dust at her feet.

She clapped once and stepped aside, pointing. Khosh Qadam bounded past her into the courtyard. I followed, trying not to smile too much.

As I poured out the bag, I noticed Khosh Qadam trailing after Mina into the mehmankhana. By the time I was done, he was already lolling on her kilim.

Mina lit the samovar, and we sat as we had the night before. The tea was even worse. The only difference was Khosh Qadam, lying all too comfortably next to Mina. She had pushed one foot into his belly, rubbing it softly and earning a steady growl of approval. I gave Khosh Qadam an incredulous look, a little wounded to have been abandoned so easily. He did not notice.

"My grandmother had one like him," she said. "Badshah. He looked after our animals and sounded the alarm at night. My grandmother, Amina, used to tell us he was actually her first husband, Nouman. Amina was very pious and she would go on Thursday nights to her favorite shrine, the grave of a Sufi who had driven the vermin and djinns out from the country's wells. But because she was so pious, she tried not to tell anyone about her habit, to keep them from praising her for her devotions and planting the seed of arrogance in her heart. After she was married, Nouman became suspicious about her nocturnal journeys. One night he decided to follow her. When he saw Amina at the cemetery with the aging mujawir who took care of the shrine, he accused her of all sorts of wild things: digging up corpses to eat them, consorting with ghouls, the like. Amina got angry then and asked God to give her creep of a husband his just deserts. Because of all her years of piety and pilgrimage, her prayer was accepted, and Nouman immediately became a dog."

I smiled. "I doubt Khosh Qadam was ever human. Too well behaved."

"He seems like it," she said, putting her foot by his head. Khosh Qadam contemplated it before offering a cautious lick. "Why are you giving me that look?"

"It's been some time since I saw someone so comfortable with dogs. People in these parts, they are different."

"He doesn't make it difficult," she murmured, going back to massaging Khosh Qadam.

That night Mina did not continue her story, and I did not ask her to. Instead she spoke more about Badshah, her family's irritable mule (Atash Nafas), the fighting pigeon her father had rescued (Mashang), sneaking out at night to look for ghouls. I offered some tales of my own in return: trying to catch fairies in the evening shadows of trees, my father's tradition of keeping horseshoes ready for the Mahdi's steed (just in case the messiah showed up at Giri). I saw Mina tense as the call for night prayer sounded, pulling us back into the now.

"Should I take him?" I said as Mina walked me out, speaking of Khosh Qadam.

"Let him stay," she replied. "There's a storm in the air."

"Do you need anything?"

Mina's hair was stirring in the breeze, and there was a faint sheen of sweat on her brow. Her expressions were always so guarded.

"Tomorrow?" she said.

"Tomorrow," I replied.

Khosh Qadam stayed with Mina. The next evening I entered her courtyard to find him sprawled out in one corner, gnawing on a string of raw meat. Mina went as she did to start the samovar. I hesitated less before following.

We fell into a new pattern. I would arrive after dusk, she and I would sit as the world darkened, we would rise with the call for night prayer. Mina always set out a cup for herself but never drank from it. She told stories of her childhood or of the places she had traveled, I would share news of the day. She did not return to the tale of her marriage. I did not press her but hoped she would.

Whatever had happened after she had wed the foreign dervish, clearly it had affected her deeply. I was bewildered by the things she had mentioned, the mysterious deaths and the blessings that had befallen our exiled people. The events sounded like something a storyteller might relate sitting in the maidan, or the stories traded by fakirs about the prophets: matters from an age not like ours, from somewhere beyond the horizon of our times. Mina, however, spoke like one giving the news.

Several days went by before I mentioned, on a Wednesday evening, that the shrines of most saints in town were open for pilgrimage on Thursday nights. There were few places where men and women might openly meet after dark, and none better than the graves of holy people. The tale of Mina's grandmother had been on my mind, and I wondered whether Mina might appreciate the same sort of nighttime adventure. Mina was quiet for an uncomfortably long time before asking me where we would meet.

The following evening, I did not go to Mina's door. Instead, when the call for night prayer sounded, I made my way to the shrine of Tor Baba, in the neighborhood of the Balkhi Gate. I lingered outside the wall until Mina appeared. Her footfalls were soft, her shawl dark. I did not know she had arrived until she stepped in front of me.

Together we entered the shrine. There were lamps burning every two paces along the wall, shedding light on the courtyard's lonely neem tree. Before us stood an unpainted dome cupping Tor Baba's grave, a drumming noise seeping out from beneath it. The sound was not of drums but the breathing of worshippers, percussive exhalations heavy with God's many names.

A new group of men entered the dome and were lost in the sound. Others lingered in the courtyard, men and women and those who were neither, chatting and exercising restless children. Some helped themselves to bowls of pulao from the large iron cauldron to the side, the rice dripping with sesame oil and strewn with chickpeas.

"Why did you pick this one?" Mina said, looking to the shrine. Her voice was soft. I could barely hear her over the pounding breaths.

It was a fair question. Tor Baba was not the grandest shrine around. There were other graves where a visitor might enjoy more blossoms, buy warding charms, partake in medicines offering a glimpse into the hidden realm.

"I like Tor Baba's story," I said.

"I've never heard it."

I smiled. "It is said…"

Of Tor Baba

It is said that Tor Baba was so devout, whenever he would see a horse being lashed by its rider, the wounds would open on his own body instead. Men and women across Persia and India heard of his miracles, pestering him day and night until he had to leave his village for the mountains, so that he could be alone with his Beloved. But not long after that, the mighty Taimur, the Lord of the Auspicious Conjunction, invaded the land.

By this time, Taimur had already stormed Persia, India, Rome, China, and the country of the Arabs. He was richer than Jamshed and mightier than Alexander the Great, and would have stormed the firmament itself if he only knew how. The last unconquered country was Tor Baba's.

For Taimur, the existence of a land beyond his control was a mortal insult. Unable to bear it, he brought hosts from all seven climes together to bring the rebel country to heel. While people argued whether they should submit or fight or flee, a woman whom Tor Baba had once saved from an unjust accusation struck out on a different path. She packed herself some victuals and journeyed up the mountainside, through wind and cold and the fangs of beasts. At last she found the holy man, absorbed in his devotions. She explained the situation and threw herself at his feet, begging him to intercede.

Tor Baba bowed his head and went quiet. Then he picked up a handful of dust from the mountains and, whispering some verses from the Quran, threw it in the direction of Taimur's advancing army.

In that moment a great dust storm howled into being, besieging Taimur's army. The storm tormented the invaders for one hundred and twenty days, blinding and battering them until they finally broke ranks and scattered. Some say the storm still wanders the earth in search of tyrants to destroy.

On the hundred and twenty-first day, Taimur opened his eyes to find himself alone, all his glory and power vanished. The Lord of the Auspicious Conjunction had become nothing. And he returned weeping to his own homeland.

Afterwards, Tor Baba came down from the mountain and settled here. He married and became a schoolteacher. He was known for his open door and open hand. But he never performed another miracle, whether openly or in secret. He had lost his bond with his Beloved. Only death could reunite them.

Above us, the night was deepening. An aging mujawir moved along the wall, rekindling extinguished lamps. A stray dog had slipped inside and a man was tossing it left-overs. The drumbeat breathing had started to ebb. Some-one inside was singing in Arabic.

"We can't keep doing this," Mina said.

I looked to her, surprised. Moonlight brushed the side of her face. A lock of hair curled out from her shawl across her cheek. Her eyes were still on the shrine but her words had been for me.

"If I have offended you..." I began to say.

"You don't understand." She turned to me, and there were dust storms in her gaze. "I am not what you think."

For the first time, I pushed back. "I knew what you were the first time I saw the tattoo next to your eye."

"That was before." Her careful expression was cracking. "Haven't you noticed how I always have you come in the evening? How I never eat or drink around you? Haven't you heard about everyone who has died since I came to this place?"

"I don't understand," I said.

"A thief. A caravan hand. Two beggars. A night watch-man." She listed them like a challenge. "There will be another tonight. Do you understand yet?"

"Those were animal attacks," I said, confused.

"Not an animal," she replied.

"What are you saying?"

"I told you, I never stay anywhere for long. Too many bodies and people begin to notice. One way or another, this is ending."

There were things I wanted to say, questions pressing at my teeth. "You can't have killed those men."

"I didn't just kill them," she said. "I fed on them."

"Mina," I started to say.

"Don't." Her mouth tightened. "All this time since you knocked on my door, it's been like a long dream. But everyone has to wake up."

Again I caught the golden gleam beneath her eyelids. I was confused and upset, wishing both that she would explain what she meant and that she would never bring it up again, that we might go back to the murky rhythm that had driven us before. But I could not find the words to give voice to that want.

Mina looked at me for a moment longer. Then she turned away, stepping out of the courtyard and into the moon-washed dark.

The next morning, in the queue for the Friday Mosque's well, I heard a pair of women chatting. A corpse had been found the night before near the Balkhi Gate, a goldsmith headed home from a shrine. His throat had been torn out and his head twisted almost wholly around. An animal, they agreed, some rabid dog that needed putting down. What else would have savaged the man so?

Chapter Three

په اندیښنو می خَان پاچا کرِ

چی سر می پورتہ کرِ ملنگ د دوهی ومہ

ناشناس

Mina stopped answering her door. I still passed her house on my rounds, and could not help the ache that sprang from the sight. I even returned to the neighborhood after nightfall a few times, looking for lamplight in the upstairs lattices or other sign of life. The house remained dark.

The days went by. I listened for rumors or news about Mina, but everyone seemed to have forgotten about her. The old gossip had been replaced by fresh stories and scandals. An apothecary's secret second marriage to a younger woman was discovered. A watchman was caught selling guns from the palace armory. A merchant's daughter fell in love with a magistrate's wife.

Some time after our visit to Tor Baba, Khosh Qadam came up to me near his old den. I knelt to rub his head. "It's all right," I said to him. "We'll get along."

But I was not getting along. Mina had come to anchor my days, and the loss of her left me with not only her absence but debris from the deeper past: memories of home, the hope that I might find it again.

Qurban Ali noticed my state but did not remark on it. I had resolved not to burden him with my troubles until after Roshana Begum's mushaira. He had been practicing with a young singer named Dawud. If he could win the favor of a woman as rich and connected as Roshana Begum, it would open many doors before him, perhaps even those of the governor's palace itself.

Prayer did not soothe my spirit, nor did my usual roving make me any less restless. I even visited Tor Baba again, seeking his intercession, but if the dead saint heard me, he was of no help. I thought about speaking to someone, some learned mullah or godly fakir, but decided against it. I did not know how to explain myself to those who had not come undone themselves.

One evening, Qurban Ali invited me to join him and Dawud for an excursion. The three of us walked to an orchard and spread a blanket under the most bent of its mulberry trees. Qurban Ali strummed the rabab while Dawud, a slight boy with a magnificent mustache, sang with a sweetness to rival his prophetic namesake's own, stitching one poem to the next.

> All my life, the heart's ties have bound me hand and foot
>> A drop of blood has dyed me from head to toe
> In fantasy's desert there is no steady compass rose
>> What need do we have to know where we are?

I returned to the orchard without them after that. The nights were hollow without Mina's company. Sometimes I took Khosh Qadam along, or rather, he would join me. It was easier to be adrift together. Maybe he thought so too.

He was with me as we walked under trees feathering the moonlit sky. There was a soft wind soughing in the branches, leaving them to rustle and sigh. From beyond rose the glow of the Khan Bazaar. Khosh Qadam raised his head and stalked off. I followed to see him approach a woman in black, the breeze playing with the hem of her robe.

Khosh Qadam had settled at Mina's feet. The moon was bright, her shadow long on the earth.

"He's been looking for you," I said, gesturing at Khosh Qadam.

"He should not," she replied. "It isn't safe."

"He's a stray with nowhere to go. Better he have a chance at a home."

The branches swayed, whispering secrets.

"You don't know how hard it is to be around you," Mina said. "To feel everything that has been lost. The hope of getting it back again. But no one can catch lightning."

"You don't think I feel it too?" I was surprised at how raw I sounded.

"You don't. You think you do, but you don't."

"What do you mean?"

"I told you what I am."

"I don't understand what you told me."

She looked away. "Proof that I should never have tried to explain."

"Then don't explain," I said. "Let the past go. Walk away from it." *And I will walk with you,* I wanted to say.

Mina touched her throat absently. "I can't do that any more than I can walk away from my own shadow."

"Sometimes I feel that way too."

"It's not a feeling," she said. "It's about what I've become." She folded her arms and one of her sleeves slipped back. On her arm was a paper talisman on a faded green thread.

"You don't have to tell me anything," I said. "But I am here if you want to."

Mina stared at me long enough that I thought she would leave without speaking. Then she sighed once, and continued her tale.

Mina

I don't know how long I spent in Dara Qala. The moment the wedding ceremony ended, the dervish's mystics took me down a passage and left me in a bridal room. It was spacious enough I suppose, and certainly laid out more richly than any home I had known. But all I saw were kilims that were not mine spread over flagstones that were not mine, quilts that were not mine piled on a charpoy that was not mine, a trunk that was not mine filled with clothes that were not mine. The only thing there to call my own was the bridal chador on my body, the fake gold at my wrists and throat. No one had told me in which direction Holy Mecca lay, so imagine, I could not even pray. I didn't know what to do with myself, I was too shocked even to cry.

Exhaustion eventually overtook fear, and I drew the quilts around myself and fell asleep. When I woke, someone had left me broth and bread. It was a hermit's food, not fit for a bride. I ate it still.

Days passed. I took to walking the castle, but there was no trace of Dara Qala Sahib, and his mystics would not talk to me: whether out of excessive regard for their master's wife or something else, I could not say. Squatting in the water closet, I heard voices from other rooms, like djinns lurking in the cracks of the walls, but the words themselves escaped me. I spent what time I could out in the courtyard, taking what sunlight there was and looking down the path toward my old home. Many times I imagined walking out the gate and back down that path, but what would my family say if I turned up out of nowhere, like a runaway bride?

"Where is he?" I asked the mystics, again and again. Husbands were supposed to see their new brides. No matter that I remembered him like a bad dream, at least his presence would have been more normal. "Where is my husband? Shouldn't he come?"

The mystics averted their eyes and gave no reply.

About a week after the ceremony, my uncle came to see me. He was in good spirits, healthier than I had seen him in a long time. He brought news of my aunt and my cousins, of Bibi Sayeda, of the small miracles gracing our people, whose noses had been rubbed in the dust for too long. He spoke to me about our people's future homecoming, of marches to further countries still.

I cut him off as he waxed poetic about the fabled mansions of Isfahan. "I want to go home," I said.

"Mina Jani," he said. "It is perfectly normal for a bride to feel sad the first time she is apart from family, in her new master's home."

"I am not sad, uncle," I said. "I'm alone here, and starting to get scared. He's left me among strangers and hasn't even come to see me."

"Bandagi Hazrat is occupied with matters of great importance, the future of our people. Look at what he has done for us. You have to trust him."

"Bandagi Hazrat?" I said. "So now he shares a title with prophets and saints?"

"Mina," my uncle said. "He is both our master and your husband. You especially have to be respectful, even more than all the rest."

"I need you to respect me too," I said.

He leaned back from me then, like a horse master before a broodmare that had tried to bite him. He said some more soothing words and got up to leave. And he did not visit again.

Maybe he would have come back eventually. Maybe I should have been more patient, or gone down to him, convinced him that something was wrong. But I was alone, I was scared, I was trapped in a strange place, and I had had enough.

I waited until nightfall to make my escape, trusting that the mystics would be asleep, and that my husband himself was nowhere to be found anyway. There was no going back home, but I still had Bibi Sayeda's talisman on my arm, and I remembered her offer, the rupiyas in her hand. If I could make my way to the lowlands, I might find work in one of the towns as a maid, figure things out from there. I never dreamed I would become one of those fallen and condemned creatures who lived in cautionary tales, but what was I supposed to do? Live alone and forgotten, locked in a castle at the whim of an absent foreigner?

From the storeroom I stole a paring knife, the blade no longer than my own palm. Little protection, but better than nothing for the open road. I thought of the stories about the governor's soldiers torn apart, the dead men in the trees. Wolves and bandits, I told myself, nothing holy about any of it.

I moved through the crumbling corridors as if I were one of the djinns in the walls, meeting no one and taking heart from that. I was almost clear when I noticed the glow from the doorway into the darbar.

If the mystics were awake, I would have to go back and try again another night. I was not about to endure a chase through the dark.

I went to the doorway and peered inside. The lamps were lit but the darbar itself was abandoned, nothing sitting on the dais but a few patterned quilts. I let myself relax, began to tiptoe back.

From inside the darbar, a voice slowly sang my name. "Mee-na."

I squeezed the grip of the knife. My palm slick, I stepped inside.

There was no one in sight. I thought I must have dreamt the sound.

"Mina," I heard again. This time from behind.

Gooseflesh swept down my arms, and I turned around.

There he was, our Bandagi Hazrat, Dara Qala Sahib. He was even taller than I remembered, wrapped in one of his fine black robes threaded with gold. His eyes were gray, crenellated by long lashes. He had high cheekbones and a brow wide enough for a grand fate. He was looking down at me, and I shook like a branch in a storm.

He drew up to me. When he smiled, my shiver grew worse.

"Mina," he said a third time. He spoke to me in slow Persian. "It took you long enough to try it."

I gripped the knife harder. "What are you talking about?" I said.

Dara Qala's smile sharpened. "I have been waiting for this night. I always wait for it, with my brides."

I needed a moment to follow his meaning. "You were waiting for me to run away?"

"You surprised me," he said. "Your folk have a history of rebellion, and I thought you would run sooner."

"What kind of sick game are you playing?"

He brushed a hand across his mouth. I was caught by the curve of his fingers, the long nails at their tips. "Since ancient times, the game of kings has always been the hunt."

I stepped back and brought my blade up between us.

"Don't come any closer," I said. I meant the words to be hard, but they came out ragged.

His expression was perfectly unbothered. "What do you think you are going to accomplish with that?"

"I'm leaving," I said.

"No," he said softly. "You are not."

"You can't stop me."

He took one step forward. "Thus spake the sparrow in the shadow of a hawk."

The blade wavered in my hand. I wanted to match his movement, to retreat, but found my feet rooted to the stone. "You are no dervish," I whispered.

"I am when it suits me to be," he replied. "As I have been guru, and abbot, and chieftain of thieves. I have been soldier and mendicant and conqueror, made feasts of emperors and saints. In me come together the greatness of East and West alike. Your mind would shatter like a clay cup trying to understand me."

I remembered how people had said his way of speaking was strange, but they had not mentioned how bizarre the words themselves were. I rallied with bravado. "A lot of talk for a man who speaks Persian like a child," I said.

"I learned the Persian language in the marble and tile of the Sublime Porte, from savants seated at the feet of the Ottoman Sultan himself. I was reciting the finest poems of this tongue before the first of your forebears borrowed a few words from it, to improve that braying speech you still use."

Despite my anger and his own, I was curious. "Ottoman? You're Turkish?"

"Turkish?" he said softly. "Turkish? Little sparrow, you know nothing of the world. You think me Turkish? Let the Turks burn." And, maybe despite himself, he told me his tale.

Dara Qala

It was the Grand Turk, the Ottoman Sultan, who stole me from my home. Robbed me in his blood tax when I was just a boy, claiming children as part of the tithe owed by conquered infidels. Devshirme, they call it in the tongue of the Turks: the collection. As if children are no different from the sacks of grain, the bolts of cloth, the swaths of stolen land.

The Sultan's troops brought us across the country and to the edge of the sea, all the way to the City on the Seven Hills, the Golden Horn, the great and bloated heart of the Ottoman Empire. They took us into the four courtyards of the imperial palace, stripped us of our clothes and our names and the better part of our mother tongues. They trained us hard in the kennels and falconries, ran us through bloody practice in the racecourses and yards. They reached for some of the boys and cut between their legs, so they could better serve in our master's seraglio. We who were left trained ever harder to escape that fate.

Twelve years old I was when I came to the Sultan's city, and twelve years I remained there, made to eat and dress and pray in the manner of my captors. Twelve years before being sent off to garrison my own country, now part of the same army that had once stolen me.

Many others shared my fate. Many others obeyed the Sublime Porte. Some had been taken young enough to have forgotten their true nature. Some preferred the Sultan's luxuries to the hardships of the past. Some even kept their state hidden, living openly as the Grand Turk's men while doing what they could in secret for their families and peoples.

But I was always shaped from different matter, a gem forged from a different mine. I would not abide by the empire that drained the very heart's blood from my country. I would not abide the stealing of children.

And when they tasked me to reap the devshirme, I threw my orders upon open flames, and walked away.

When the Sultan sent his legions for me, I thought my people would rally behind my cause. That my fellow stolen boys would wake up from their long slumber. That the priests weeping from the pulpits about the loss of their children would bless my war with holy water. That the nobles would shuck their sloth and remember something of our people's old glory.

But the Grand Turk's gold was stronger than the bonds of blood. My rebellion ended almost as soon as it began, in one night of fire and steel in the marshes, my small follow-ing broken under the boots of Sultan's men. I barely escaped the battlefield with my life, running into the tangled trees. It was there, bloodied and tired in a high grotto dripping with shadows, that I found the stryge.

I had heard rumors of him before, the ancient witch who took blood in exchange for favors. I knew what I had to do. I crawled into the grotto and opened my veins, poured out what little was left in them. Watched him take shape from the shadows. Begged him to hear my grievance.

And the stryge offered me a bargain. He would take all that I had, and I would either gain the power to conquer my oppressors or perish. I told him if I could not defeat such monsters, it would be like dying anyways.

Few survive the turning, but I was one of them. And after waking anew in the bosom of the earth, how could I ever doubt my destiny again?

I stepped out into that first night of my second coming drunk with power. I could have passed through the camps of the enemy and burned them to ashes, even walked into the Sublime Porte and ripped the Grand Turk's head from his shoulders. But I thought to go to my people first. To give them hope of freedom, to renew our land once more.

So I called them to me, the rabble and the great alike. I met them in the halls of my forefathers, and when the sun had vanished and the holy warriors had gathered, I revealed what I had become. Gave them the vision of what we could now be, under my banner and my guiding hand.

And I stood there in shock as they cursed me for a mon-ster, drawing their swords. And I wept as I stepped into the fray, bathing myself in their blood.

And when it was over, in the bodies of my people, I glimpsed for the first time the truth of all things.

Mina

Now, I will not pretend that I understood everything Dara Qala said. All I knew of the Ottomans was that they were a mighty kingdom who bred Arab horses, and maybe they were Turks. I had never heard of blood taxes or witches living in shadowy caves. What I did understand was the pain tinting Dara Qala's voice, the longing that clouded it. In that moment I thought him no different than us, someone who had fought for his people's well-being and suffered exile as the reward. I began to say so.

My husband stepped closer still. The motion was startlingly animal, as if he were uncoiling instead of walking. "It has been a long time since I told that story," he said. "If only you had it in you to understand. But you never will."

His words were a wind and they blew out my budding sympathy. "Stay back. I am leaving, do you hear me? I don't want to be with you. I don't want this."

His shadow engulfed my body, his breath brushed my skin. "And why," he said — and I could feel the force flowing through each word — "why would it ever, in the unspooling of eternity beneath the firmament's primordial gaze, matter what you want?"

"Let me go," I said. "Just let me go."

He had drifted close enough to fill my vision. The lamplight limned his jaw, ran across his cheekbones, fell into his eyes, but much of his face was plunged into shadow. I could feel my heartbeat in my fingertips. I realized I was holding my breath.

"Let you go?" he said. "Little sparrow, I will take all that you are."

I steadied my hand, and drove the knife into the side of Dara Qala's throat.

He flinched.

I stepped back, breathing hard, hardly able to believe what I had done. The words I'm sorry flew to my lips and hovered there.

Dara Qala smiled.

His fingers curled around the hilt of the knife. When he pulled it free, the whole blade was dripping. With his other hand he reached for me, pushing my hair back from my neck to expose the skin. The charnel house smell of him filled my nose. I was shocked by the intimacy of it, could not fathom the sight of him taking the blade from his own throat, and the confusion held me fast.

Dara Qala parted his lips and I watched his canines grow into fangs fit for a wild beast. I felt a line of spit fall warm on my skin, the heat of his breath close behind. The smooth power in his hand as he pulled my head to one side.

The fire ripping through me as he bit into my throat.

The pain came so hard and so fast, I couldn't even scream. It felt like I was being choked. There was a gurgling sound coming from somewhere, but I could not say if it was me making it or him as he drank me into the dark.

I was never supposed to wake up, I know that now. He took his fill from me, the bastard foreign djinn, the stryge, and he tossed the rest away like garbage, thinking nothing of it.

But I did wake. I woke on the earth outside the castle, robe torn, left for the crows and wolves. I remember the cold sweat on my limbs and heat under my skin, the ache branching down through my body and ringing in my teeth. I watched the sky lighten and wondered if I was dying.

But I got up.

That was how I left Dara Qala: alone, bareheaded and barefoot, wrapped in tatters, stumbling down through the dark. The morning sky felt like fire against my eyes. I made my way to Bibi Sayeda's door, lucky that nobody had spotted me on the road. I rapped on it with an unsteady fist, and when Bibi Sayeda opened up, I folded into her arms.

She hid me for days, saying nothing to anyone. I never asked to see my uncle or the rest of my family. They had given me over to that monster, and though they could not have known his nature, I did not know how to forgive them. For her part, Bibi Sayeda made her home my own. She tended to me, trying to build my strength with soup flecked with herbs, taking twilight walks with me in her courtyard. She never pressed me to talk about what had happened in the castle. In the nights she never left my side, sleeping in the same bed, looping an arm around my waist and pulling me close.

My memories of Dara Qala were a tangle of bad dreams. I tried to convince myself that what I remembered was nightmare, not memory. But then I would touch my neck and find the scabbing wounds there under my fingertips.

An animal attack, I told myself, which would explain the fever afflicting me. Yet that could not explain the fear that locked my tongue and sent tremors through my limbs at the thought of my husband.

Soon I was reduced to a constant shiver, mind wracked by wavering dreams. All I had for succor was the talisman Bibi Sayeda had given me. I would press my nose into the paper, trying to smell the musk she had daubed onto it before my wedding, the same perfume she liked to wear, but I could smell only blood.

"You still have it," she said one night, touching the green thread.

I threaded my fingers through hers. "It worked."

She did not say anything in reply, holding me as I shook.

But I was lying. The talisman had not worked. The sunlight was starting to bother me. What began as headaches in the courtyard during the days quickly turned into painful blindness, then the feeling of fire crackling under my flesh. I stopped going out before dusk entirely.

Worse still, I could not stomach any food or drink, vomiting whenever I tried. As my fever worsened, my body began giving off a bloody scent. Bibi Sayeda lied to me about it, telling me I smelled fine, but every so often I caught the look on her face. She gave up trying to feed me. I spent days on my back, too weak to move.

Bibi Sayeda grew convinced I had been struck by the evil eye or possessed by a djinn. Too late, I tried to explain that Dara Qala was actually himself a djinn, but by then I was in no state to explain anything. She thought I was raving.

One evening, Bibi Sayeda put me on the back of her mule and brought me to a faraway mosque. It was kept by a mullah of discretion and good taste. When the mullah came out, he examined me up and down before declaring that a devil had settled in my body. The only possible remedy was an exorcism.

Bibi Sayeda stayed outside while the mullah lit a flame, over which he placed a tin laid with wild rue seeds. He rubbed sainted dust across a pair of willow switches, telling me to lie back. I obeyed him in a daze. When the seeds began burning, the smoke made me start coughing.

I tried to tell the mullah to wait, but he was too busy reciting something. I struggled to speak, something alarming and strange swelling in my mouth. A drumming noise drowned out the mullah's words. He struck me with the switch then, over and over. As he did, I gave in to the thing unfurling inside me.

The mullah's switch went up and my hand dragged him down, teeth bursting into fangs as I gouged his throat.

Only after I drank my fill did I come to my senses. My fever had broken, my thoughts were clear again. I was sprawled atop the mullah's corpse like a beast. A scream and a sob coiled together in my chest.

And it was there, with blood on my mouth and an ache in my heart, that I recalled Dara Qala's tale. I tried to push the memory away, as if I could force myself to forget, as if doing so would change things. But it was too late. I could almost hear him speaking that foreign word, naming what he was, what I too had become, the stryge.

"I went to Kabul after that," Mina said. "Visited every physician who would see me, prayed at every shrine I could find. Begged God and the living and the dead to let the hunger pass, to make it so that my strange appetite would not last. But it came back. It always comes back."

I felt as if I were waking from a confusing dream. I could not make sense of Mina's tale. It sounded like madness. But in the moonlit orchard, hearing the way her voice was drawn taut, I could almost believe.

"How did you come from Kabul to here?" I said.

"I stayed there for months," she said. "Hoping for some sort, any sort, of answer. The city was suffering after the war, but there were still many scholars and friends of God there. I would have stayed longer if I hadn't felt him."

"Him?"

"It was like a second heartbeat. A tremor under my veins." Mina shook her head. "I thought I was imagining things until I saw one of Dara Qala's mystics roving the streets. I ran that same night and didn't stop until the feeling left me."

"You think he found out about you. Came after you."

"I know he did. I barely escaped him at Kaniguram, had another near miss in Chaman. That's why I always keep moving. I can never stop. It's like he told me. He won't let me go, not until he takes everything first. He is a man who would be king, and the game of kings is the hunt."

"What about our people? Someone among them will help you. Your Bibi Sayeda, certainly. Others too. You could be safe with them."

"Even if that were true, they would not be safe from me. Just like you aren't."

I let out a long breath and glanced up at the night sky. Out in the orchard, the stars were almost as they had been in Giri, when I had looked up at them as a boy. It had been so long since I had seen home.

"You don't have to leave," I said.

Mina did not reply.

I pressed her. "I will stay away if you want me to. But I hope you'll let me come by."

"Why?" she said, almost savagely. "After everything I've told you, why?"

"You do not know?" I said.

"I told you, I cannot stay."

"You choose not to stay. There's a difference."

Mina gave me a hard stare. "Then what? I keep on feeding until people start suspecting their problem isn't a feral dog? I wait for some righteous neighbor of mine to call the kotwal to my house, saying I'm a whore? You and I keep on with these moments in the dark until Dara Qala comes to finish what he started?"

"So instead you'll just go on to the next town and do this all over again?"

"No," she had said. "I won't be doing this again."

Khosh Qadam got to his feet and shook himself. Let out a low whine.

Mina started back out of the orchard. She did not stop me when I fell into step with her, but neither did she speak.

Chapter Four

جانانه خه الله دي مل شه
زه شینكی خال او زلفي تا لره ساتمه

ناشناس

Qurban Ali missed our regular Friday meeting. I waited in the cafe after prayers but he never showed up. When I asked the owner if he had come by, I was told he had not been there in days.

Qurban Ali owned a modest house down a narrow lane, the sort of place where one was too easily trapped behind overburdened mules. The walls were dappled by the occasional shadows of sour orange and olive groves. The smell of them swirled in the air with wood smoke.

It took Qurban Ali a while to answer his door. When he did, he was thin and wan, eyes red with exhaustion. Even so, his smile was true. "I am fine," he said, in reply to my blunt query. "I lost track of time, that's all."

Dawud was there too, shy in his reply to my salam. Qurban Ali did not try to excuse the boy's presence by claiming he was only there to practice for the mushaira, and I felt a rush of affection for that lack of comment. The silent acknowl-edgement marked our bond even as I began to sense that my friend had stepped across a threshold, that he was moving across a new horizon.

We went to sit on his roof, sharing a bowl of dates and almonds. From there we had a view of the Khan Bazaar and the palace beyond. Spread before us was the dun expanse of town, damasked by sunlight and softened by shadows, adorned by the muted green of dusty leaves. I smelled the wine on Qurban Ali's breath.

"Something's changed with you now," I said.

Qurban Ali smiled. "And with you, my friend. For some time. Yet you won't tell me about it."

I looked away. "I met a woman from Sher Khan's people. I've been spending time with her, and wanted to keep doing so. But she is leaving."

Qurban Ali put a hand on mine. "Ah, Sado. I am sorry."

"She's right to do it," I said. "There is nothing here but the past."

"You are not the past, Sado Jana."

"Am I not?" I said. "Certainly I'm no future."

"Of course you are," Qurban Ali said. "You are still breath-ing, and you are still you. That is enough."

"Not for her," I said. "Maybe not for me, either. Look at me, Qurbana. Wandering around a town that will never be mine, smiling into the faces of people who would mount me on the gibbet if they only knew."

"If you see the bared teeth of a lion," Qurban Ali recited, "do not think that the lion is smiling."

"Who said that?" I said.

"An ancient Arab who wasn't that different from you,

my friend. He too spent time in the prisons of kings, and dwelt in their shadows after. But he spoke truly. You are who you are. And a lion's teeth will always be fangs."

"Lions live with their own," I said. "I'm apart here."

I found myself telling Qurban Ali what had happened, or enough of it. I said nothing of djinns and stryges and Mina's own claims of drinking people dry. Strange as such things were, they were not what weighed down my thoughts.

"Jana," Qurban Ali said, sighing. "Your heart is bleeding. And if you do not face her a last time, I worry that it will only keep doing so. You need to go, my friend. Find a better ending for your tale."

As the daylight fell away, I went to Mina's door. Despite Qurban Ali's counsel, I had almost decided against going. It was not anger but embarrassment that gave me pause. Had I pleaded so shamelessly with anyone else, it would have been bad enough. Before Mina, I felt I had lost what little dignity was left to me.

She was right, I told myself, as I made my way into the streets around the Gulistan Gate, the call for prayer staining the air. I had no right to ask her to stay. I did not know what to make of her story. There were times I suspected she was a madwoman, perhaps one driven to murder. I could not even blame her, after what our people had suffered. In other, quieter moments, I was less certain. But it did not matter. Perhaps we were bound only through a moment in time that had long since ended. Perhaps our paths had branched apart before we ever met.

I was so absorbed by my thoughts, I did not realize something was wrong until Mina's door swung open under my knock. The neighborhood's usual quiet suddenly felt ominous. I hesitated, then stepped inside.

The courtyard was silent, the mehmankhana unlit. Khosh Qadam was nowhere to be seen. The fear climbed up through my chest that Mina had already gone until I looked to the upper story. There was lamplight there, seeping through the lattices and spilling through an open door. I made my way up and followed the glow.

Mina was standing before the window at the far end of the room, its gauzy curtain restless in the breeze. The kilim at her feet was patterned in red and gold leaves. Upon it lay a man.

He was older, beard shot through with gray, body beginning to slacken at the shoulder and waist. From the cut of his leather sandals and plain robe, I guessed him to be one of the nomads passing through town on their way to the melas of India. No bonds tied him, but one of his legs was bent in a bad way. There was a plea in his eyes, the same look the sheep gives the butcher as the blade presses in before the cut.

"I wanted you to see," Mina said. She looked slightly unraveled, as if she had been freshly exiled from the gardens of paradise. "Before I go."

"Mina," I said, but I did not know how to continue.

"I never told anyone the whole story before," she said. "There was never anyone to tell. I wanted you to know that I told you the truth."

"I believe you."

"No you don't." Something broke in her voice. "No one

does. Even Bibi Sayeda never accepted what I told her about Dara Qala. A liar, an opportunist, a conqueror, a foreigner, a fiend, but never the nightmare I know him to be. The mullahs and fakirs all told me the same thing. They said that God creates all things with a single nature, that the natures of creatures cannot change. That one born human will die human, that one born an animal will die an animal, that one born a djinn will die a djinn. One never becomes another. A wolf raised among humans does not become human, they said. Everyone I trust with my story thinks I've gone mad. The only ones who really know, who have no choice but to know, are the dead."

"I've tried to understand," I said. "All this time."

"I know." She stepped forward. "This is what I can give you for that."

"The only thing I want from you is your company."

"You won't want it. Not after you see the truth."

"I don't believe that."

"You will." It was almost a whisper.

Mina's fingers curled in the nomad's hair. With one hand she dragged him upright, neck pulled back to bare the thick vein branching through it. Her lips peeled back from her teeth. In the lamplight, I watched her canines lengthen into fangs fit for a wild beast.

Mina plunged her fangs into the nomad's neck. The man gagged, eyes lolling like a man possessed.

Mina closed her eyes and drank. The shadows deepened around us and the silence with them.

When she was done, she let the corpse fall to the kilim with a thump, a slack huddle of cloth and flesh and bone. Mina paid it no heed. She was looking at me, dark eyes shining, blood bright upon her mouth.

"Look," she said through gritted teeth. "Tell me you know what you see."

I took a step closer. It felt as if I were wading through a dream. I heard a faint ringing in my ears. Qurban Ali's words echoed through it and I repeated what he had recited to me. "If you see the bared teeth of a lion, do not think that the lion is smiling."

"So you know," Mina said, the end of days in her face, "what I really am."

"The first time I saw you," I said, soft as a dove's call, "the moment I saw the tattoo at your eye, I knew what you really were."

She nudged the nomad's corpse with one foot. "A murderer."

I did not look away. "I can say the same."

"It isn't the same."

I stepped closer still. "I know what I know, and you know it too. We were never strangers."

"You cannot possibly have known about this."

Slowly, carefully, I made my way around the corpse, coming to stand before her. The iron tang of her clouded the air.

"This does not change anything," I said.

"How?" she whispered.

I reached out slowly, newly aware of the blood coursing through my neck. Mina watched me, unmoving. My fingers brushed the corner of her mouth, traced the line of her jaw.

Her hand curled against the front of my robe, bunching the cloth. She pulled me forward and pushed her mouth onto mine. Her lips were still warm. Beneath them, for a moment, I felt the hard curve of fangs.

Then she had my lower lip between two rows of very human teeth, holding it like a grape, the skin begging to be burst. She bit, and my blood dripped into her mouth as my arms locked around her.

Chapter Five

که منصور غند په دار و په سنګسار شم

نشته دا چه ستا له مینې توبه ګار شم

حمید

In the morning Mina was gone. She had left in the dark to carry the corpse away, and I had lain down in the mehmankhana to wait, but my eyes had shut from exhaustion before her return. I woke to see dawn fluttering against the curtains, almonds and quince slices nearby where Mina had doubtless left it. I was already late for my daily rounds. I realized that I did not care.

I washed up and stepped outside. I had not slept in such a large building since prison, and that had not been so empty. The cistern was dry and Khosh Qadam was curled up in it, gnawing on a string of meat. I joined him.

It occurred to me, standing in the grand and hollow home, how lonely Mina's existence was. I had always imagined myself something of a recluse, but compared to her, I was rich in friends. She hardly saw anyone save the strangers she found in the nights, and they did not count as company. Khosh Qadam and I were the only fixed points in her days.

I thought of venturing out but dismissed the thought. People would notice my strange coming and going from Mina's home. My mere presence was an offense. The kotwal and his men would not be merciful, and even less so if they learned who we both were, where we were supposed to be. Mina, I thought, would be less merciful still.

So I spent the hours paging through the handful of tomes on display and playing with Khosh Qadam, until the shadows grew long and the afternoon was ready to surrender to dusk. I looked up to see her standing in the mehmankhana's door. She waved in greeting, fresh hesitancy in the gesture. I went over.

"You didn't eat anything," she said.

"I'll eat at the mushaira tonight," I said. A thought came to me, and I added, "Come with me."

"To the mushaira?" she said.

"The host is a woman," I said. "I've heard she always makes room for others too, on the balcony and roof."

"It's sudden."

"I promise it will be worth it."

Mina considered me. "I'm not planning to leave without saying anything, you know."

I did not say I was not thinking of that, for I would not lie. "Even so. Come out and see."

She relaxed a little. "I've never been to a mushaira. Some men in Aghazpur would go to the hujra at night to share verses, but girls were never allowed in with them. I liked it better when storytellers passed through."

"Why is that?"

Mina's lips twitched. "Because I was allowed to go hear them."

"Sometimes there are storytellers in the Khan Bazaar. A few set up their rugs in the maidan, and even the ones in cafes are usually audible from the street. You could hear them again."

"Maybe." Mina seemed ambivalent. When I gave her a questioning look, she went on. "It's hard for me to feel with the stories they usually tell. I used to imagine myself as Laili, Gulandam, Badri Jamala. Outwitting suitors, chasing after lovers, bargaining with djinns. But I can't see myself in them anymore."

"It's hard for me too," I said. "Still, they are our stories."

"They were," Mina said. "But they're not made for what I am now." She must have noticed my expression, for she added, "Maybe a mushaira is, though. Tell me where we are going."

I left her before sunset, keeping enough time to wash up at the hammam. By the time I stepped out, the early stars were piercing the heavens' dome. I stopped at the Friday Mosque on my way. The mullah's litanies there were sad and slow. I stood in the back of the congregation at the last of the etched and gilded pillars. As I put my brow to the ground, I whispered not the Arabic words of the prayer but my own pleas.

Roshana Begum's home was in the neighborhood of the governor's palace. It was the finest part of town, shot through with wide alleys sprinkled with water. A trellis ran down the road on which her mansion stood, jasmine hugging its posts, brightening the night and perfuming the air. I had no way of knowing if Mina had come and could only hope she had.

When I named myself as Qurban Ali's guest, the doorkeeper ushered me into a grand courtyard, the walls lush with arabesques. The patterns had been traced over with talc so that the lamplight lent them a silvery glow. The center of the courtyard was spread with overlapping kilims, artfully arranged so that each weave kissed at least two others. The men sitting atop them wore elegant turbans and filigreed robes. From behind the balcony's teakwood screen drifted down the murmur and sway of women. I took up a spot at the courtyard's edge.

One after another, the poets advanced for their appointed moments. Some recited while others sang. Only a few were accompanied by musicians. Cupbearers slid among the patrons between performances. I accepted a cup but did not drink from it. I did not know how Mina felt about wine. A strange worry, perhaps, given what I had seen her do.

A spritely old man in a white robe smiled and walked away to a round of adulation. Qurban Ali and Dawud came up to take his place. The former caught my eye and smiled quickly before he addressed the assembly.

"What you are about to hear are my words and also not," he said. "The gift of this poem is from the blessed martyr Mansur Hallaj, but though he composed it in Arabic, Dawud and I have brought it into Persian for you to hear tonight. Of course, there are those who say poetry cannot be translated. May you disbelieve them, at least for a moment."

Qurban Ali sat and laid his rabab across his lap. Dawud lowered himself as well onto his knees, head bent and hands folded. I saw Qurban Ali tilt his head and take a breath. The tune he struck was dark and full. I found myself falling into it as Dawud sang.

So kill me and set fire
    To these crumbling bones of mine
And when you pass my remains
    Among the graves gone to seed
You will find my beloved's secret
    Folded in the hollows of what is left
Bring together the pieces
    Of all that luminous matter
Of wind, of flame
    Of sweet water
And sow them all in a land
    The earth of which is but lifeless dust
Set to watering them
    From rounded cups
From serving girls
    From running streams
And when seven days have passed
    A perfect plant shall have grown

I looked at the balcony as the song spun to an end. I could not see Mina, of course. But I wondered if she had seen what I had: the glance shared between Dawud and Qurban Ali, one gaze, just long enough, as their performance closed. There were secrets in that glance, and more than that, hope of home, found anew.

I did not get to speak to Qurban Ali. His performance had drawn attention and there were many now who wanted to meet him and Dawud. I sat instead at the common dastarkhwan among the flock of chatting guests, helping myself to a few morsels here and there from the heaping platters of bread, rice, and all sorts of garnished meats. No one noticed when I got up and left.

The happy sounds of the mushaira fell away on the street. My head was spinning from the simple intoxication of so much company. I looked around but did not see Mina. We had agreed to meet at an appointed corner after the performances. We were far enough from our own neighborhoods that we could risk walking together, at least for a time.

I did not hear her until she was already next to me. She moved surely through the night, her ease almost animal in nature. I was noticing it as if for the first time.

"I thought you might have left," I said.

She arched her eyebrows. "Are you still worried about that?"

I smiled.

We fell into step, heading away from the palace. "Your friend is very good," she said.

"I'm glad you enjoyed it."

"More than I thought I would," she said. "I had almost forgotten."

"What people do," I said.

"Yes."

We continued a while in silence. The streets were all but deserted. The town might as well have been a ruin. Perhaps in another hundred years, it would be one in truth. Something moved in a nearby alley's shadows, likely a passing stray.

"I am leaving," she admitted. The words fell on me like the executioner's sword. Before I could say anything, she continued. "All this time I've never left these lands, where I could hear our tongue and walk under the shade of our trees and pray at the shrines of our saints. They're not our own country, neither the old nor the new, but they still feel a little like home. I knew that if I was ever to escape Dara Qala, I mean really escape, I would have to go further. They say God's earth is vast, and maybe it's vast enough for me to lose him, or him to lose me. But I was afraid. I thought that if I really left, if I was off in some foreign country where I knew nothing around me, I might lose the last bits of myself too, and become him. So I lingered, going from one town to the next, just like the little sparrow he said I was. I couldn't bring myself to go off to a new world alone." She halted, fingers locking around my wrist to stop me too. "But maybe if I was not alone, even if I were somewhere else — then maybe it will be like your friend sang. Maybe someday, my seven days will pass too."

I felt light enough to fly. "All you needed was to ask."

"No," she said. "It should never be like that. I've seen what that leads to."

"This," I said, "is not that fate."

"This is exile," she said, "And I never wanted you to turn exile for me."

"We are already exiles," I said. "Our country is the rebellion tattooed at the corner of your eye. We'll never get it back. But when we're together, it's not yet gone."

"How do you know that will be enough, when you're somewhere far away?"

"Because I know why I kept coming to you," I said. "Because for the first time in far too long, I can remember who I was when I answered Sher Khan's call. I can remember who it was I hoped to be. If we walk apart from each other now, I'll lose that again. And I do not want to."

Mina lifted her head and took a step back. Our hands drifted apart.

"It would have to be tomorrow," she said. "I've already stayed too long."

I thought of Qurban Ali, of the glance he had shared with Dawud. "Maybe I have too."

"We'll be running. It won't be safe."

"Every soul tastes death. The trick is doing so with some dignity."

"Don't talk like that."

"Like what, one of Sher Khan's fighters?"

"You don't know what those slogans led them to."

"It does not matter what they became," I said. "The two of us are still who we are."

Mina looked at me a moment longer. A man was walking down the street in the opposite direction. He murmured a passing salam and I returned the greeting. Mina's gaze flickered toward him before coming back to me.

"I should have never opened my door," she said.

I smiled.

As night spread its wings, I took Mina to my own home. It was only a room above some shops, rented with half my usual earnings. If even one person had seen Mina come up the stair with me, the whole street would be on fire with gossip by noon.

By then, it would not matter.

Though we would be leaving almost immediately, I was still embarrassed to show Mina into my quarters. There was nothing to adorn the room but a charpoy laid with a striped quilt and a narrow window overlooking a poplar tree. I went over to the latter and shut the curtain, tying it down.

The room was on the old maidan, a remnant of the town's first flourishing, most of which had been destroyed when the Mongol army of Genghis Khan had passed through this land. Where the Friday mosque and house of government had once stood, a cattle market now reigned. Even at night the smell of hay and dung lingered in the air. From the window one could see the remains of the old mosque, one wall and the stump of the minaret, no taller now than the thatch roof of the cattle shed next to it. Some people said there was a cellar under the wall where the prophesied Mahdi was hiding, waiting for the day when God would give him permission to come out and defeat the oppressors.

When I looked back at Mina, she had unfolded my prayer mat and lain down. I did not disturb her as I headed back out.

I felt almost weightless without my water carrier's bag across my back. My steps were unbalanced in the best way. I had abandoned all my clients yesterday and would never see them again. Even now, I thought to myself, they would be wondering where I had gone, cursing my name for leaving them dry. They would be fine. There were others who could do my job. But no matter what came next, I was done with that phantom life.

It took me some time to reach the neighborhood of the Gulistan Gate and get into Mina's house. If any of her neighbors were watching, the uproar about public morals would fuel conversation for a month at least. The thought brought a smile to my face, which grew when Khosh Qadam trotted up to me. I knelt to hug him and he whined into my chest. I squeezed his jaw and promised him something to eat soon.

Mina's long saddlebag was right where she had said it would be. There were clothes, and quilts stashed in it, a few mohurs too. As I fastened the ties, I thought of how many times Mina must have done exactly this, getting ready to run alone.

I regarded the house: the tapestries and the kilims, the samovar in the mehmankhana, the tiles painting the cistern, the air thick with remembrance. I knew Mina had been sincere when she had offered it to me.

"Come on," I said to Khosh Qadam.

Morning was brightening the world as we reached the Khan Bazaar, the roads coming to life. The shopkeepers were opening their doors and neighbors exchanged greetings from the rooftops. A water carrier was making his way up an alley, announcing himself in bored tones. A woman was singing from one of the rooftops. I could not make out the language.

One of the nomads was setting up her stall, frying up a first batch of lamb on the karayee. I bought some and threw pieces to Khosh Qadam as the stores opened, sitting under a mulberry tree while he happily gnawed away.

Under the gaze of a toothless old merchant in his alcove, I picked through an assortment of colorful burqas: orange cotton with golden calligraphy running down its edges, green and blue silks threaded with flowers, simple white sheets set with silver mesh. I thought of Mina's preferences and settled on a gray burqa with maroon needlework spidering along the chest and sleeves.

I could not tell if Mina approved when I handed the garment over. She only unfolded it and slipped it on, adjusting the edges. I could see nothing of her face in the shadows under the mesh.

"It will keep me moving in daylight," she said. "But I won't be very useful."

"You cannot stand the sun at all?"

"The only blessing in that," she said, "is that neither can he." I did not have to ask whom she meant.

By the time we came out, people were bringing their animals into the cattle market. Many were nomads, selling the excess of their herds before beginning their autumn march. Others were farmers in from the near country, trying to get rid of the animals they could not afford to feed through the cold months. It was from the former that we purchased a pair of felt saddlecloths, and from the latter that we bought two aging mules, who ignored Khosh Qadam weaving between their legs.

That is how we left: the two of us atop the mules, a gazelle hound loping alongside. We took the road south out into the country. The path broadened and the houses behind us fell away until we found ourselves on the open plain. The foothills were shadows on the horizon, the last of the summer fields washed by sunlight. A narrow track branched from our road to slice through them. It was said it ran down towards the sea.

Perhaps people would notice my absence, spread rumors of seeing me with Mina. Perhaps Qurban Ali would hear them, would wonder what had happened when I missed our next meeting. I felt a sting at the thought. But he was crossing his own horizon, and I had to cross mine.

"You didn't bring any weapons," Mina said. Her voice was strained. Even sheltered by the burqa, the sunlight was taking its toll.

I gave her a small smile which I hoped she could see. "I thought there would be no need for weapons, traveling with you."

"I told you, I'm not much use in daylight."

"Maybe I think I have no need for any weapons to defend us, either."

Mina paused. "My uncle and my cousins took pride in their arms. Many of the men I knew did. Especially when the King forced us to give them up. Holding onto their weapons, it was like holding onto their dignity."

I stared at the foothills. The afternoon wind was picking up, dust peeling off the road and dancing across our path. For the first time in years I felt myself heading into the future. That, I think, was what let me speak of the past.

"I was never a soldier..." I said to Mina.

Sado

I was never a soldier and never wanted to be one. Other children made fun of me for it in Giri. As I grew older, the teasing turned to whispers that my Hindu mother had thinned my blood. Even my father worried.

The only one who understood was our mullah sahib, a graybeard who loved quoting Sheikh Saadi and who fed all the village dogs right in the mosque. As the years passed, I found myself spending more and more time with him. When the King's taxmen announced that we now owed them not only earnings but labor, Mullah wrote a fatwa declaring the corvee unlawful, and read it out at the local council. The soldiers came and hung him after that.

Mullah had wanted me to go to school. A real one, not the mudbrick room where he taught the basics of Persian and how to recite the Quran. In his own youth, he had gone to the great colleges of India, but the wars there had made the roads dangerous. Still, he had insisted I find a way to travel and learn, that the earth of God was vast.

I do not know what Mullah would have made of my fate. I never could ask his opinion of Sher Khan's rebellion. Plenty of mullahs objected to the uprising. They went around telling people kings were God's own shadows upon the earth, staying quiet about the salaries they took from the same kings. I imagine Mullah would not have agreed with them. But I think he would have been sad even so.

The moment Sher Khan and his band rode into Giri, calling for us to join him from under the great plane tree, I stepped forward. Everyone knew who Sher Khan was, what he was doing. Many spoke admiringly of him even then, boasted that they would ride at his side. None of them moved to answer his call. They all looked surprised when I did. I hardly noticed. I was too busy remembering

Mullah's slack jaw, his shorn beard, his robe torn all the way down the middle as his corpse swung from the same plane tree's boughs.

My hands shook all through my first battle. It was a night raid on an army stockade, we were hoping to make off with some horses and guns. I was made lookout. Sher Khan's party had only just reached the corral when one of the King's soldiers spotted me. I had a black gun on me, I had never used one before. I fired and missed. The soldier's return shot grazed me. He came after me with steel then, and I could not reload in time, had nothing else to hand but a saddle knife. I was not a soldier and I did not want to be one. I will never call myself by the name. But I learned, then, what it was to fight.

The wind was still rising, pushing at us from the side. There were shade trees lining the path, planted by some prince from a distant age, whose charity gave travelers respite across the ages, for which his memory was continuously blessed. The boughs bent and groaned under the gale, as if a cavalcade of djinns from the hidden realm was passing through, trampling the branches under invisible hooves.

"A strange season for wind," I murmured.

Mina pulled to a halt.

I drew up next to her. "What's wrong?" I said.

"Listen," she said.

For a moment I heard nothing out of place. Then I caught it, the sound woven into the wind, a low moan coming out of the north.

Mina sat completely still, burqa fluttering around her body.

"Mina?" I said softly.

"It's him." Her voice had gone taut as a drawn bow. "He's here."

The hair rose on my skin. I felt a tremor between my backbone and my ribs.

Dara Qala was coming.

Chapter Six

اذان پہ خَنڈ کوہ طالبہ

زہ د جانان غیرِبي تہ اوس ورسیدمہ

ناشناس

Once, in ancient times, long ago, all the country's saints
met in a dream to discuss the fate of the world. The angels
had brought a new command from the heavens. The king-
ship of the land was to pass from our own people, and go
into the hands of a new sovereign appointed by God, a
windblown prince named Akbar. The saints sorrowed
for their people but accepted the order, for they could
do nothing else when it came from the Truth itself. But
one of them, an old man named Sheikh Lodi, refused to
obey. How could the God he loved send such a fate upon
his people?

The other saints begged Sheikh Lodi not to argue. "The
best of people, the Prophet Muhammad himself, accepted
the harshest commands of the Almighty," they said. "You
too must be content with what we are told." But Sheikh
Lodi was not content. No matter how hard he tried, he

could not bring his heart to bow in submission to what heaven had decreed.

It did not matter in the end. Akbar's army rolled over the country like the monsoon floods. People died, from among both those who yielded and the ones who fought. Matters eventually settled, as they always do. Sheikh Lodi's protest was for nothing. Akbar exiled him from his home.

On his way out of the country, Sheikh Lodi found himself suffering under the summer sun and took shelter under a spreading plane tree. When he recovered, he thanked that tree for giving him shade, and blessed it as a refuge for those who might need it in times to come: a refuge, he prayed, that would be stronger than what he himself had given his people. The prayer was accepted. In time, travelers began gathering under that tree. Some people built a low wall. Others heightened it. A kitchen was built, then stables. That, they say, is how the Grand Caravanserai came to stand on the trade road: a refuge sprung from a sorrowing saint's prayer.

By the time we reached the Grand Caravanserai, we needed the refuge. The dust storm had swept down upon us from the foothills, and the edifice's two stories of sun-dried brick were blurry in the haze. Mina had her head lowered against the grit and we had to keep dragging our mules back onto the path. Khosh Qadam was a mere shadow at the edge of my sight. The tall wooden doors, carved with Solomon's seals, were already halfway shut.

The doorkeeper ushered us in without greetings, closing the gate behind us. He was an older man, dragging one of his legs as he led us across the courtyard. Two wolves were tethered near the stalls for the merchants' baggage and animals, under the meager shelter of an awning. Khosh Qadam's ears ran flat at the sight of them. I quickly swung down to pull him back by the neck. The wolves, already agitated by the dust storm, rose and growled. The doorkeeper was no less anxious, saying something to Mina I could not make out over the gale. She shoved some mohurs into his hand to calm him.

We tethered the mules with some difficulty, but refused to leave Khosh Qadam in the stall with them. The doorkeeper grew upset once again, saying we could not bring a dog into the upstairs rooms, that other travelers used the room, respectable folk who knew the angels shunned places where dogs had slept. Mina handed him more coins to resolve the debate.

Once inside, the walls muted the gale enough for us to hear each other speak without shouting. We were led to one of the upper rooms with an iron lattice overlooking the courtyard. I roped down the shutters as Mina brought the lamps to life. The room was clean, the wall flecked with old paint, the floor spread with a sheepskin mat. Khosh Qadam padded around its shadows, then curled up in the one he decided was best.

Mina pulled off her burqa and collapsed on the charpoy. Her hair was disheveled, the shadows around her eyes deeper than usual. I knew the same layer of dust on her skin was shining on mine.

She caught my look. "I told you," she rasped. "I don't do well in the sun."

I poured some water. "Drink."

"I only bathe with water," she said. "It's not what I drink."

It took me a moment to follow her meaning. When I did, I put the cup down and bared my forearm.

"What are you doing?" Mina said.

"What needs to be done," I said.

"You don't understand."

"I understand that you are about to collapse, that's enough."

"No, it isn't." She was watching me like a hunting falcon. "You don't know the effort it takes to control myself. To keep myself from reaching for every person around me when I feel hungry. To have kept from reaching for you all this time. If we do this..."

"If we don't," I said, "then this journey will have ended less than a day's ride from where it began, with your enemy getting closer as we speak."

"I don't know if I can stop."

"You'll stop," I said confidently.

Mina pursed her lips. "It's too risky."

"I heard," I said, "that they said to every woman at the encampment the same thing, the night before the end, before they took the needles and ink to their eyes."

Mina went quiet for a moment. "I never thanked you," she said at last.

"For what?"

"For never asking why I did it."

I sat next to her and brought my wrist up. "I never had to," I said.

Mina's fingers curled around my arm to steady me. Her lips were warm, a soft burn on my skin. There was a bloom of pain. I looked away for her sake and mine alike. It did not take long for the sound of the gale to grow distant.

I heard a whine in my ears, steady and high. The world began to seem more suggestion than reality in my gaze.

"Sado."

My eyes snapped open. Mina was knotting a strip of cloth around my wrist. I had never seen her looking at me quite so alertly. It took me a moment to realize it was concern.

"I'm fine," I said. "Are you?"

"Better." She paused. "Thank you."

"It's nothing that needs thanks."

"Yes," she said, the blood on her lips bright as her eyes. "It does."

The gale howled on. We had no way to move while it did, and the only consolation was that our hunters were likely trapped too. There was no choice but to rest. I stayed until Mina closed her eyes, then went downstairs.

The Grand Caravanserai's kitchen was humble, the cook throwing cumin into a simmering iron pot. She ushered me into the hujra with the rest of the patrons. There was a single dastarkhwan laid out in the room. Most nights, travelers would eat in the courtyard under the stars.

There were a handful of others already there, clustered at one end of the dastarkhwan. They returned my salam and made room. When the cook came out with lentils and seeded bread, I was too parched to swallow even the idea of the meal. I asked for some rosewater sherbet instead, draining the cup at once and savoring the cool of it. I quietly asked the cook for more and listened to the men speak.

They had come in with a caravan from Persia, a mix of merchants and porters and camel drivers. The group already passed through a string of glittering cities and were bound for Lahore before turning homeward. They needed little prompting to share their adventures: a close encounter with river bandits, a drinking game picked up in the garden of a prophet's tomb, the unexpected blessings brought by a piece of raw meat hurled at them by a naked fakir on the road.

I listened to the roster of their travels with growing anxiety. I only knew the places of which they spoke through news and legends. Yet here I was, heading toward a future shaped by such distant lands. Shaped by distant lands, I reminded myself, but also shaped by her.

The caravanners got up afterwards to wait out the dust storm in their rooms. I washed up and did the same. When I entered, Khosh Qadam lifted his head, and I tossed him some purloined bread. Mina was motionless on the charpoy, a red chintz snarled around her. I lay down on the sheepskin on the floor. Sleep closed in, despite the gale.

A weight on my chest pulled me back awake. Outside, the wind was still battering the walls. I opened my eyes to find Mina kneeling atop me. Looking up at her in the gloom, thoughts still mixed with dreams, I remembered childhood stories of the mouthless djinns that came at night to steal sleepers' breath. And I remembered that Mina was a different species of creature entirely.

She had the chintz twisted around her shoulders, even though the heat brought by the dust storm had seeped into the room. I tried to read her face, worried that what I had given her before had not been enough, that she had yielded to some deeper instinct.

Mina's nails brushed the side of my face, her hand a question against my jaw. The chintz shifted and I saw she was bare beneath it. Only then did I know. We had barely touched one another after that first hungry embrace. Even after we set out together, I had kept myself from dwelling on the question. I had thought she had too.

I did not move away. Mina's touch grew more confident. Her hands drew the robe off my shoulders. I bit down panic as they did, pushing away the better part of my memories about tangled limbs, of dust and knives and gritted teeth as I pushed to take life before my own was taken from me. So many times I had been this close to another's body during the rebellion, and so very few like this.

Mina leaned back to look at me. I wanted to retreat before her gaze, to apologize for my sweat and my frame and the scars here and there on my skin, puckering my flesh where bullet and blade had found me. Mina shrugged the chintz down, her thigh pressing mine, warm as a fever.

I sat up in answer. She wove her legs around my waist. One of her hands curled into my hair, and my fingers gripped the back of her neck as she pushed herself onto me. Our breath entwined as the gale roared on outside the Grand Caravanserai, pounding at the walls, hammering at the doors, rattling the shuttered windows. And we two ignored the storm.

After, lying together drowsy and flush, I found myself listening to the wind's rage. It had never sounded so impotent. It felt as if the future was unfurling within me, something I had not sensed since the days of Sher Khan, or maybe even before then. I thought of Mullah's recollections of his travels in his student days, of the grand cities and colorful melas, of the time he had roamed with a caravan of bric-a-brac traders and laid eyes on the sea. He had so badly wanted me to do as he had done, to seek knowledge even if it took me to China. When they hanged him from the plane tree, they killed that desire along with him. The only future I could feel after that was Sher Khan's dream of a new world, one where beasts of labor threw off the yokes of obedience, where those suffering feet on their necks might rise up and become kings. Yet that night, sheltering from a storm in a caravanserai grown from a prayer, I felt I had traveled the course of the uprising not for Sher Khan's dream, but for the moment in which I was dwelling right then, the life that now lay before me, one born from everything I had not said to Mina, everything I did not need to say.

Mina groaned in her sleep. Her eyes fluttered under their lids, her limbs were shining with sweat. I felt her shivering against me. I realized that I should not have been able to hear her over the gale. The wind had gone slack.

I touched her arm. "Mina."

Mina's eyes snapped wide and she bolted upright, breathing hard. Her hand fell on my thigh and squeezed it savagely. I bit back a yelp of protest.

Mina ignored me, looking to the window, the wildness in her face swiftly turning to worry.

From the courtyard below, the wolves began to howl.

Soundlessly, Khosh Qadam came to his feet. The two wolves were making enough noise for an entire pack. The cries were long and high, almost keening. This was neither the baying of beasts on the hunt nor a warning call.

Theirs was a sound grown from fear, and I felt that same fear closing my throat.

The wolves went quiet. Silence rolled through the Grand Caravanserai.

In the courtyard, a voice sang out, rich and deep, stretching out a single word.

"Mee-na."

We came down in the dark. The Grand Caravanserai's passages were deserted. There was no trace of either keepers or guests. It was as if no one had ever been there at all.

Mina and I stepped out into the courtyard, Khosh Qadam padding at our heels. The world was aglow with starlight. A party of men ringed the open space, heads shaved down to the skin, swathed in mantles of fringed wool despite the heat. They watched us but we were not watching them.

There was a man there, and he was the night. His face was the moon, pallid and distantly beautiful. His black robe was the dark smeared across the heavens. Where the cloth brushed his skin, it sounded of the susurrus of the evening breeze in the wheat fields. His eyes were the burning conjunction of the two unlucky planets. His smile was bright and cold as the firmament. The dust quivered underfoot as he took a step. When he moved, it was like no other creature I had seen. There was a deep certainty to his walk, one reserved for saints alone. He only had eyes for one thing.

"Little sparrow," Dara Qala said. "It is good to see you."

"I don't feel the same way." Where his voice was strong, Mina's was simply terse.

Dara Qala's seemed unbothered. "You will come to feel differently, in time."

"No," Mina said. "I won't."

"You think so now," Dara Qala said. "But when one hundred years pass, when the last person who knew your first life has turned to dust, when you have drifted across the terrestrial plane and found yourself more rootless in each new country: then you will ache for the company of one who can truly know you."

"You never knew a thing about me, and you never will."

"Oh?" Dara Qala drifted closer. "I know part of you feels ashamed of how you feed. I know another part thrills at the power of it. I know you left your home to guard those you care for from yourself. I know you left because they could never understand you. I know you have been so very alone."

"Stop telling me how I feel," Mina said, "and tell me how to turn back."

"Turn back?"

"How to become human again."

"Why would you ever want to do that?"

"Because I'm not you," Mina said. "I never asked for this. I never wanted it."

"But some part of you did, even if you cannot understand it." He drew closer still. "I have voyaged the world for generations, and I can tell you with certainty that precious few come back as you and I have."

"So what?"

"So you are special, Mina. A pearl of the ages." Dara Qala took another step. "When I turned, I was the first in the lifespan of an empire. I have hoped longer than you can comprehend for someone like you."

"You didn't think me so special the night you drank me dry," Mina said.

"When I took you for a bride, it was from an ordinary stirring. Had I known that within you lay a shard of existence so akin to my own, that night would have ended very differently."

"I was a girl," Mina said. Her voice went ragged. "I was hopeful. I was scared. I was not your pearl of the ages and I am not that now."

"You do not fathom your own value," Dara Qala said. "Come with me and learn it."

"I know my exact value," Mina said. "It's written at the corner of my eye."

For a flickering moment, Dara Qala hesitated. He had not understood what she meant.

"You are confused," he said. "I too once saw myself as monstrous, the way humans see us. You feel as you do because you are like an animal who has suddenly become human, but still sees itself as a beast. In the eyes of cattle, all humans must be monsters. Let me help you see yourself as you should."

"I can see better than you think," Mina said.

"Little sparrow, you do not yet have an eye that has seen centuries pass."

"Is that how you excuse everything you do? You've lived too long to care?"

"The likes of us need no excuses," Dara Qala said. "The sooner you accept that, the easier it will be for you."

"You're shameless."

"The only freedom is in living without shame."

"I am not interested in your freedom," Mina said.

"You are already free," Dara Qala said. "All you have to do is realize it."

"The only thing I need freeing from is this curse you've forced onto me."

"Even if it were possible, I would never give you up."

Mina's hands curled into fists. "When are you going to understand that I am not yours to give?"

There was a flicker of displeasure on Dara Qala's face. "Perhaps I spoke too soon when I called you poor quarry, back in the highlands. Even I am growing weary of this hunt."

"Then leave me alone."

Dara Qala gestured at the mystics spread through the courtyard. "Look around. You do not need to be alone."

"I'm not alone," she said.

For the first time, Dara Qala turned his stare on me. I was aware of even the sweat clinging to my eyelashes.

"He," he said, "is not the company you need. And you are not his."

Dara Qala gestured and his mystics moved forward. I stiffened. Khosh Qadam growled.

Mina stepped in front of me. "Don't."

"We must," Dara Qala said. "And you will understand in time."

"I'll come," she said. "That's what you want? I'll come."

"Mina, don't," I said.

She ignored me. "You want me in your company? Fine. I'll come. But let me have what you have. Let me have someone of my own."

"Is that what you think he is?" Dara Qala said.

"If you want me to be like you," Mina said, "then I should act like you do."

"I could simply take you back right now," he said. "You could never stop me, and you know that is true."

"But you don't want me taken, do you?" Mina said. "You don't want me as quarry anymore. You want me to come. And I will, but only if he comes with me."

Dara Qala considered me, his gaze passionless as a corpse. When he looked back to Mina, an amber light flared to life in his eyes. He gestured and the mystics fell back.

"Take him, then," Dara Qala said. "So long as you remember your own place, little sparrow."

I started to protest. Mina turned, laying a hand on my chest. My heartbeat was pounding a drumbeat into her palm. I would not be the fetter that imprisoned her. I would sooner fall in battle, so she might at least run.

With her other hand, Mina pushed a lock of hair back under her shawl. As she did, she brushed a finger against the corner of her eye, a sign so subtle and swift, I might have imagined it.

I could only trust that I had not.

"Good," Dara Qala said to her. "You are learning."

Mina gave me a last glance, then looked away to him.

Chapter Seven

جانانه هسې وخت به راشی

چي توپک واخلو لاس تر لاس سنګر ته حونه

ناشناس

We rode.

Our band was twelve souls in all, moving slowly. I rode with Dara Qala's mystics, though I went more lightly than they, the great bundles on the flanks of their mules being enfolded in colorful wraps and heavy carpets. In our midst were two camels, a howdah swaying like an elephant's trunk atop the larger one. The being inside was imprisoned under the flaps until every sunset.

Mina had refused a howdah of her own, riding the second camel alongside Dara Qala in silence, sheltered by her burqa. I watched her from my place in the train, Khosh Qadam walking by me. We had not spoken since the Grand Caravanserai. I had not gone near her, wary of Dara Qala's eye, and she had not come to me.

At the end of the second day, the mountains sharpened into view. Mina lifted her burqa as we settled the animals and pitched tents, drifting out to the camp's edge. Her expression was as inscrutable as it was under the veil. But the way her footsteps took her toward the rising country, it was as if she was being drawn up to it, like water coming up from a well.

By the following afternoon, the ground underfoot was swelling into the mountains and pushing us onto the heights. It was stark and empty country, the occasional farm or flock coming into view only to fade just as swiftly. The one steady presence was that of our own party.

The mystics held themselves apart from me, but they did not feel entirely like strangers. I recognized the way they moved, the tension and edge of a hunt run long. I had shared the same mood often enough during the rebellion, out too many days and bringing back too little game, running myself lean on the long way around to strike at the King's encampments, searching fruitlessly for comrades who were never coming back. I saw, in the mystics' knotted stances and focused stares, the same urgency for relief after hardship. I could not say what they saw when they stared back at me.

Around the evening tents, they shared food with me but little else. They met even small talk with brief and uninviting answers. Even among themselves, they spoke mostly in murmurs and soft chatter. I stopped trying with them quickly enough and simply watched them camp and decamp. They kept saddlebags for pillows, unwrapped their mantles for blankets, rested their hands atop motley weapons: saddle-hatchets and knives, rugged maces, javelins with short hafts, simple swords. They held themselves all the while as if strangers to the world.

I looked to those weapons and faces, and wondered if we had once fought together under the shade of Sher Khan's pennant. Wondered if I had once known any of them before they had scraped their heads clean and wrapped themselves in wool. Wondered if I would have shaved myself just the same had the shape of my life been different, had I not stolen away from the long march early and put myself adrift on the plain, had I been made to gaze upon the wreck of my people, for whose lost future I had bled.

Who was I to think the mystics strange?

On the fourth morning, I looked to Mina as she drew down her burqa and got ready to ride. For better or worse, I was not as the men around me were. The force of new belief had not yet torn me from the fabric of my past. Mine was an older and fainter faith, though it still had some power left.

So I hoped.

The road grew steep and narrowed into a cattle track. Our band fell into a file, keeping Dara Qala and Mina at the core. As we twisted and turned up the mountainside, a pitted wall came into view, perched on the edge of a sheer drop. It could not be the castle from Mina's story. That lay in higher country still, where the remnants of our people had been sent. Even so, the place felt almost familiar from her tale. How many haunts, I asked myself, did the devil have in this land? Over how many broken hearts did he hold sway?

We followed the track higher and higher until the ruin took shape before us. The wall had crumbled at the entrance and the doors had rotted away, making a toothless mouth of the gate. Our band crossed without ceremony into the courtyard, where arches rippled along the gallery. There were sacred figs growing there but their limbs were mostly stripped, though it was too early for leaves to fall. Faded rags and pennants had been stuffed into the cracks of the walls, markers from past pilgrims who must have thought this place a holy one. At the far end of the courtyard was a darbar, the front wall sheared away by time or conquest or maybe both, leaving the hall exposed to the elements.

I dismounted with the mystics and tethered my mule with theirs. One of them tried to tie up Khosh Qadam as well. I stepped into his path, and he backed down.

When I looked back, the howdah was empty, the flaps hanging loose. I glimpsed the edge of Mina's burqa disappearing into the shadows of the darbar.

I so longed to know her thoughts. Our bond had begun as a fraying thing, but we had managed to weave it thicker in one another's company. Now he had come, with all the force of holy revelation falling on an unsuspecting heart, and what did the sparrow do when it fell into the shadow of a hawk?

One of the mystics was approaching. "Bandagi Hazrat calls you," he said.

Dara Qala's title was smooth and strong on the mystic's tongue, and at last I understood their distant manner. I had spoken Sher Khan's name the same way once, using it to hold back everyone who did not. How else could

I force myself forward in a war against people with whom I could have sat knee to knee, had my fate been but slightly otherwise? How else but through that name, and all that it stood for, could I keep from drowning in the blood I had spilled?

But nobody had spoken Sher Khan's name like that in a long time. And there was another name sounding around me now.

I nodded to the mystic and followed him into the darbar. Khosh Qadam padded after me. Behind us, the day burned down towards the dark.

He sat at the end of the darbar, where the evening had the least reach. The broken roof's shadow sliced a line across the dusk-washed hall, an impalpable shield against the dimming sun. The mystics had put up a seat for their master and draped it with the same kilims upon which they slept, laying others at his feet in a makeshift court. They were patterned with spreading trees, ivy and blossoms, reeling birds, and other motifs beloved by the weavers. Dara Qala watched from atop the assemblage of woven tales. Mina was nowhere to be seen.

The men retreated. Dara Qala weighed me in his eyes.

"Why are you here?" he said softly.

I hesitated. What was I supposed to say? Mina and I had never put it to words.

Dara Qala leaned forward. When he spoke, the words held the weight of resurrection day. "I have uprooted the masters of your country as if they were weeds. I hollowed out the caravanserai in which you cowered singlehand-edly. I have held the necks of kings' daughters in their own harems. You will answer."

"She and I share a past," I said.

"You share a past," he echoed. "But not a future."

I did not know how to reply to that.

"You amount to so little." He spoke without rancor. "You are dust and water held together for the blink of an eye, and then you fall apart, no different than rotting chaff. But I am true flame, white fire burning hot across the ages. When the last person to have known your name is devoured by worms, I will still be as you see me now. And so will she. She thinks now that she cares for such matters as you, but time blots out all ancient sentiments. I am not making an argument, I am disclosing to you the truth of all things. When you are eternal, the only thing that matters is the eternal. And as I am eternal, so is she."

I felt as if he had his hand around my heart. "Why are you telling me this?" I said.

"For your sake," he said, "for her sake, walk away. Leave. Let her accept what she is. Her past is dead. If you care for her, do not stand in the way of her future."

I stared at him like a stunned horse. As he painted the future, I could almost see it. My body under the dust of some far country, Mina rootless and windblown above it.

Khosh Qadam brushed against my leg. A memory came to me then: an evening in Mina's sitting room, her foot pushed into his belly. She had not been smiling, but something in her expression had been achingly close to peace.

"You will not," Dara Qala said, "go unrewarded."

The pressure in my chest fell apart.

He wanted me gone. If he was right, if he and she alone were eternal, all he had to do was wait. But he wanted me gone now.

He would not want that without reason.

"Do you understand what I have said?" Dara Qala said.

I met his gaze more evenly than I had dared to before. "I will go," I said. "When she tells me to go."

Despite the murk, I caught the flare of his nostrils, the sudden glow lighting up his stare. In that moment I knew what it was like to be the worm under the sparrow's eye.

"You are a fool," he said. "She will not tell you to go. Before she does, she will have turned her teeth on your throat, and the last thing you will know before being drained to a husk is how wrong you were. She will turn. You may not think it, even she may not think it, but it is inexorable. I know it. I know it better than anyone else ever could, for there was a time once when I was her. The only difference is that I was alone, and she — she will always have me."

Dara Qala looked past me. "Remember that I offered you mercy," he said. "Remember that you chose this."

I followed his gaze. The mystics were forming an assembly. Coming forward through them was Mina.

She was as lovely as a bride, walking along the edge of the roof's shadow, limned by twilight. She had set her burqa aside for her robe alone, and the breeze played with its hem. Her eyes glimmered against the gloom.

Dara Qala beckoned. She came to his side wordlessly.

"It has been a long road," Dara Qala said. "Shall we break our fast?"

Mina made no protest. He took her silence for consent.

Dara Qala rose, the dark itself shifting around him as he did. One of the mystics approached and knelt, back straight as a spear, feet folded beneath him. The mystic pulled the robe off his shoulder, the stance taken with the care of the devotee in the mosque who measured each press of his brow to the earth between two flattened palms.

Dara Qala cupped the mystic's jaw in one hand and turned his head aside. He bent near, body curving across the mystic's until the latter was all but swallowed up. I caught the glimmer of bared fangs before he bit down. The mystic shook in his master's hold: from ecstasy, from pain, from something of both.

Dara Qala straightened. The mystic swayed briefly and came to his feet, with less grace than before. Even as he moved off, another mystic approached to offer himself.

I watched Dara Qala take him the same way, then a third. A fourth. A fifth.

I looked to Mina, but she had eyes only for Dara Qala, watching him drink his fill.

When it was done and he had settled back on his seat, Dara Qala shifted his attention to Mina again. "You wanted someone of your own here," he said. "It is only fitting that he offer you your due."

Mina looked to me at last, not at my face but my body. Despite all that had passed between us, I could not hold back a shudder. Even Khosh Qadam stiffened next to me.

I stepped forward. Slowly went to my knees.

Mina mirrored Dara Qala's motions, stalking forward. I wanted her to talk to me, wanted to hear her voice, to trade even once glance, but she did not meet my eyes. She made as if to take my arm, as she had in the caravanserai.

"No," Dara Qala said. "That is not the way."

Mina's mouth tightened. She hesitated.

I reached up and pulled my robe aside. Before she could turn my head by her hand, I looked away. Pain speared through the spot where my shoulder met my neck, and I could not hold back a gasp. It was as if someone had driven a burning blade into me. She took from me with no hint of her earlier care. The darbar blurred in my eyes.

Then she was gone in a snap of black cloth.

I got to my feet, shaking. The floor seemed to be swaying underfoot, as if it too had been unbalanced.

"Now do you understand?" Dara Qala said. He was staring at Mina with fresh urgency. "Can you grasp what I have been holding out to you? You will never go hungry again, little sparrow. Never again will you be alone. There was a time once when you thought me a foreigner. But you will find as the years pass that you too are forever foreign, no matter where you go, unless you choose to walk in the company of your own."

You are not alone, I wanted to say. You have never been strange. But I did not speak, and Mina was still looking at him.

"I know this better than you can imagine," Dara Qala said. "You were not wrong before. I am a stranger and have been one for centuries. Time and time again, I have tried to build a place for myself. Time and time again, I have watched each one crumble and burn at the hands of ignorant mobs, beings so much lesser than you and I. I know, like you cannot yet know, that there is nothing for us in this world without each other. No existence more precious than alongside one's own kind. You think I am hunting you. Mina, I am trying to save you from decades of heartbreak and pain. I am trying to offer you a home."

Mina tilted her head.

"Open your eyes, Mina," Dara Qala said. "What you think a curse is the greatest gift, if only you can accept our nature. Think what might be if we come together. We alone can stand above human quarrels. We alone can bring authority to those who need it. Offer sanctuary that cannot be breached. We alone can establish peace among creatures through our strength. I have ruled many petty kingdoms, but I do not wish to rule for myself anymore. With you at my side, we could do more." He paused. "In time, we could even build our own tribe."

"You are right," Mina said at last, and it was as if she had struck at my throat again.

Dara Qala's eyes flashed triumphant.

"You are right," Mina repeated. "I never wanted to accept my nature. What you made me. But you are right. I don't have a choice anymore."

"You are home, little sparrow," Dara Qala said. "You are with your own."

"I am with my own," she echoed.

She stepped up to his seat, her hand brushing his. Dara Qala's fingers curled against hers. Mina moved to his side, staring out with him toward the mystics gathered in the sunset, toward me among them.

"I heard something once," she said. "A line from an old poem, told to me on a night when I was struggling to accept what was before me, what I had to become. I am not struggling anymore."

Mina bent and placed her lips to Dara Qala's ear, as if to tell him a hidden thing. But her voice was clear, and her gaze finally flickered up to meet mine.

"If you see the bared teeth of a lion," she recited, "do not think that the lion is smiling."

Mina bit into Dara Qala's throat and tore away. Blood arced dark through the twilight.

My heart sang.

The mystic next to me had a dagger in his waistband, and I spun to grab it while he was still staring in shock. Before he could react, I drew the dagger and brought it down on his chest. Pain and fear bloomed on the mystic's face as my hand grew warm with blood. I looked back at him with my spirit in tatters, the dead cry coming back to life on my lips. "Sher Khan!"

But it was Mina on my mind as I pulled out the dagger and stepped into the fray.

I have seen cavalry riders hurl javelins through hoops at full gallop, seen marksmen bring down high-flying cranes with their black guns, seen wrestlers slam one another in dusty arenas with the force of falling stone. I have seen soldiers move together under fluttering pennants and the beating of drums, seen boys whip their locks as one through the evening sword dance. I was never a rider, soldier, dancer. But I knew how to dance even so.

I reached the next mystic before he could draw his weapon and cut into his neck. He gurgled and sagged against me. I shoved him to the ground and flew on. My dagger flashed as I blocked and parried the mystics' knives and spears. My feet fluttered over the darbar's stone as I slipped the looping swings of their maces. Khosh Qadam wove between my steps, snapping at the mystics' heels, herding and hunting. Around me flowed a river of outraged voices and eyes sparking with wrath. I let myself drown in its current.

I swung the dagger and cut a deep gash into one mystic's arm. He dropped his sword to cradle the wound. The anger drained from his eyes like wine poured out from a cup even as I drove my blade under his ribs. The mystic fell and blood pooled under him. A flash from the corner of my eye caught me and I dropped under another man's cut. As I came back up, a punch caught my mouth and I staggered. The mystics swooped down on me with ready blades.

Mina's hand exploded through one of their necks. The man gaped in disbelief, lifeblood bubbling from the ruin of his throat. One of his comrades was faster than the rest, his axe coming up. Mina turned and grabbed the front of his robe, yanking him close with fangs already bared.

I hurled my dagger at one of the mystics and snatched up a fallen sword. Two of them fell back before my relentless cuts. Khosh Qadam crossed before me to drive back a third. The mystics' resolve was wavering. The blade in my hand sparked against theirs as it arced high and low. Blood spattered the floor of the darbar as it gouged one man's thigh. I stepped toward his companion and felt steel punch into my side.

The mystic who had speared me pulled out his javelin. I fell to one knee, pain flaring through me. My fingers went weak across the hilt of the sword. I could hardly keep my grip, much less bring up the blade. The pain held me better than fetters as the mystic prepared the killing blow.

Mina grabbed the javelin out of his hands and snapped it in two. The mystic looked up as her slap caught his jaw, and the crack of his neck breaking echoed across the darbar. Mina whirled to face a man standing alone. He took one hand from his mace and raised an open palm to shield himself, to submit, to plead. Mina was on him in a single bound, driving her thumbs into his eyes. The mystic's scream came out ragged. Mina wrapped her fingers around his skull, lips twisted. Bone crackled between her hands and the mystic's head shattered to pulp.

A shadow fell over her.

Dara Qala gripped Mina's throat and lifted her up with one hand. He was so much larger than her, black robe fluttering in the evening breeze. The remains of daylight only accented the looming dark of him. His skin was flecked with his own blood, his robe agleam with it.

"Little sparrow," he said through his teeth.

Khosh Qadam ran at Dara Qala's legs with a red snout, and bit his ankle.

Dara Qala lurched, more surprised than hurt. But he lost his footing all the same. His hold loosened just enough for Mina to wrench free, gasping for breath.

Thunder swept Dara Qala's features and he drove one foot into Khosh Qadam's side. There was a snap, then a whimper.

Mina rammed her shoulder into Dara Qala, driving him across the line of the roof's shadow, out of the darbar and into the courtyard's evening glow. Dara Qala caught Mina and pulled her out with him. The two stumbled apart.

Dara Qala narrowed his eyes against the dusk, turning back for the darbar. Mina stepped into his path.

Every stone in the ruin held its breath, the tattered pennants and dead trees too. The darbar was scattered with trampled kilims, dropped weapons, torn robes stirring over torn bodies. The mystics were fallen and I was all but down among them. The sun was nothing more than embers smoldering on the edges of the mountains. The first stars were glinting in the heavens above.

Dara Qala stepped forward, and Mina struck.

She raked her nails across his face and snatched at his neck. He shrugged her off like water and lunged with a lion's grace. She clawed at his stomach and tore long lines in his robe. He stamped at her legs hard enough to crack the stone underfoot. They circled one way and then the next.

A smile was growing on Dara Qala's face. He came at Mina with sudden lurches and false starts, swinging open palms one moment and fists in the next. Mina gave way before every foray. I had seen her drop men before me the way men swatted flies, and she could not take even one of Dara Qala's blows.

Gritting my teeth, I forced myself up, fingers barely clinging to the sword. With my other hand pressed to my side, I started to limp forward.

Dara Qala's moves were growing ever more confident. He drove Mina as he wished, forcing her further back, towards the darbar. She came at him again each time, trying to keep him in the courtyard, away from the shadows. But not even the failing light and the wound in his neck were hampering him now. Again and again she rushed him, and he seemed almost lazy as he pushed her away. She could not bring him down. And all he needed was to reach the dark.

Dara Qala's fist snapped out and Mina moved too slowly. The punch landed square on her chest and sent her reeling back across the shadow line.

I caught Mina before she could fall, pain branching through my body. Over her shoulder, I saw Dara Qala step back into the shadows. Mina looked up at me, hair disheveled, eyes bright, and I pressed the sword into her hand. Her fingers curled around the hilt as Dara Qala reached out for her once more.

Mina spun and drove the blade into his heart.

Dara Qala faltered, wobbling back from Mina, slowly stepping back out into the courtyard. For a moment I thought he might simply draw the blade out like an unwanted thorn and keep coming on.

He collapsed to his knees, bewilderment painting his face.

Mina walked out into the courtyard and grabbed the sword's hilt. Dara Qala lifted his gaze to hers, started to raise one hand. Mina wrenched the blade free and he gasped. He started to speak.

Mina screamed into Dara Qala's face and swung, cutting his head from his shoulders. Blood burst from his trunk across the fading day.

The corpse swayed at Mina's feet. Slowly, almost gently, it began to fall. As it sagged, the evening light took hold of the ancient flesh and seared it. By the time the body struck the stone, it was nothing but crumbling ash. The silk robe fluttered down like a collapsing tent.

Quiet took hold in the courtyard, broken only by Mina's breath. She dropped the sword and stepped back. Her chest

was heaving, her face shining as the daylight finally vanished, and I did not know if it was blood shining on her
skin, or tears.

Chapter Eight

و نحن اقرب اليه من حبل الوريد

قرآن

Mina bound my side. She tore a long strip from Dara Qala's robe for a bandage, and I gasped as she knotted it tight. There was blood dusting my torn lip, more seeping from my neck, but I could find no hunger in her face.

As soon as she finished, Mina went to the smallest form among the fallen. She knelt and laid a hand on Khosh Qadam's flank. I made my way over more slowly. Each breath was like the press of a burning brand. Before I could ask, Mina looked up with relief.

She ripped another bandage ready and put her hands on Khosh Qadam's foreleg. There was a murmured apology, a deft twist, a sharp whine. I stood lookout as she wrapped Khosh Qadam's limb, trying to keep my eyes open.

When Khosh Qadam's leg was set, Mina took hold of one of the fallen mystics and carried him into the courtyard. She laid him there in the moonlight and gently straightened his limbs, turning his face in the direction of Mecca. I gathered what she was doing and I moved to help.

We made funeral shrouds from Dara Qala's kilims, drap-ing the nine dead mystics with fine weavings. The court-yard wall was already crumbling and we pried stones free to weigh down the makeshift cairns. From the barren trees, the flags and ribbons watched us work.

I was arranging one of the corpses' limbs when I stum-bled, suddenly lightheaded. I caught myself with one hand and realized I was trembling. The dark at the edge of my sight was not from nightfall alone.

Then Mina was there, easing me back. Her lips were moving but her voice came as if from afar, and I could not catch the shape of her words. Nor could I control the shaking.

I had seen this fate in the rebellion, from a bullet to the stomach or a blade across the ribs. I knew too well how it could end. There were things I needed to say, things I wanted Mina to hear. I opened my mouth to speak. She put her hand over it.

The next time I looked up, it was to a twilight expanse of desert. Through eyes half shut, I beheld myself lashed in place atop a mule, bent over across its back and moving through the waste. Before me rode a woman in a rippling gray burqa. She glanced over her shoulder through her grille. I could hear nothing but the beating of my own heart.

The desert wavered in my eyes, Mina as well. In place of them, arcades of unlovely red stone shimmered in and out of view. The dust and sweat mixing atop my skin, even the dull fire under it, were all too familiar. I had felt such a fever before, in the prison where I had been held at the rebellion's end. When I looked down at my hands, I could see manacles looping across them.

That is how I made the journey, passing through delirium and dream, trying to keep the sight of Mina in my burning eyes. The prison yard crackled at the edge of my vision, threatening to overwhelm day and night alike. It did so in the end, plunging me into phantasms of my old captivity, pulling me through the raised fists and flung stones until I cried out for relief, eyes snapping wide open.

I found myself lying on a charpoy in a dim room. I was bare but for the bandage around my chest, limbs tangled in a quilt. I was bedraggled from head to toe from sweat, but the heat inside me had gone.

The side of my face was wet like the rest of me, but sticky too. I turned my head to find Khosh Qadam licking me awake.

Khosh Qadam limped back as I eased myself upright. There was a fresh robe folded next to the charpoy, along with a pitcher of water and squares of sweetened barley. I ate and drank slowly, washing up with what was left.

I still heard a faint pulsing, steady and soft and deep. I had thought it my own heartbeat at first, but could not throw off the feeling that it was now coming from somewhere outside of me.

I rose and Khosh Qadam struggled up as well. His leg was swathed in a bright kerchief, his motions halting, but he seemed alert enough. I fed him what was left of my meal and scratched him. He allowed this only as long as it took to finish off the scraps, then padded over to the door. I opened it and he slipped out.

I followed Khosh Qadam into the evening, entering the sparse garden of the house we were in. A stair ran up the side of one wall to the rooftop. Khosh Qadam was waiting expectantly at its foot. A thorn of pain dug at my side when I picked him up, but it was bearable. The drumming noise was growing louder.

We came onto the roof and Khosh Qadam tumbled out of my arms. I looked out at a town I did not know, huddled in the shadow of different mountains and feathery palm trees. All before me glimmered the source of the sound I had been hearing, too grand for me to grasp in full, something I had never before seen but knew from a hundred stories.

I was looking at the sea.

Khosh Qadam's movement caught my eye. He made his way over to an abandoned dovecote, the mudbrick stained from ages past. Mina was sitting in its shadow, facing the froth and foam of the waves as they beat the shore. Khosh Qadam settled next to her. I went to her other side and did the same.

"You look terrible," Mina said.

"And you look lovely," I answered.

"Only because I've fed well," she said.

Together, we gazed at the coppery sky, the same light pressed into the waves. There were feluccas out on the water, sails curved wide. The shapes onboard them hauled up the nets as the prows turned towards the shore. In the distance, someone was singing: one of the fishermen, or someone waiting for them. The melody blended into the cries of birds wheeling overhead. Summer was coming to a close.

"I was so careful at first," Mina said. She pushed some hair off her face. "About the people I took. I promised myself I would only feed on men who put their hands on me. I kept my word too, at first. But by the time I met you, I had long since stopped caring. I was so hungry, all the time, and I didn't want to be. When he said I never had to go wanting again..."

I took her hand. Her fingers coiled through mine.

"Do you know what I hate most?" she said. "All this time on the run, I never had to imagine what it would be like to actually live on like this. Everything was about how to flee, how to fight, how to feed."

"And now?" I said.

"Now," Mina said, "all I can think about is why, of all the unfortunates across all the centuries whom he bled dry, the only one to turn stryge was me."

"We don't know if you're the only one," I said.

"Does it really matter?" Mina said. "I came back like he did. I grew the same hunger he had. Something in me is the same as something in him."

"So?"

Mina gave me a look. "So I don't want to be like him."

"You're also unlike him," I said. "You flew from him. You fought him. You stopped him. You chose a different path."

"For now," Mina said. "What happens if someday I give in?"

"Remember this," I said, "and don't."

Mina shook her head. "As if it's so easy."

"It might not be easy," I allowed, "but you are not doing it alone."

She shook her head. "You don't get it."

"What is it?"

Mina kept her eyes on the sea. "When we were back there in the ruin. When he had me drink from you. I could see it:

the future at his side, never hungering again. And I didn't know what I was going to do until I did it."

I considered her before replying. "Do you know how they punished us after the rebellion? The fighters, I mean."

"Only rumors," Mina said. "No one wanted to talk about it."

"They made us stone each other," I said. "In the prison. It took a long time for the King to decide what to do with us, and the soldiers were angry and bored. I have this dream about it. I saw it again on the way here."

Sado

In the dream I am walking into the courtyard where they let us out during daylight hours, the only escape from the overcrowded cells. But instead of other captives, I see an old man sitting in the shadow of a plane tree. His face is sad, his hands cupped in prayer. I step closer and the dust motes around him are rising in a golden whirl. From that churn, the mirage of the Grand Caravanserai grows around the sorrowing graybeard.

I start walking toward the caravanserai but then see another man in the corner, thin and dark. His robe is caught in a wind that always blows for a hundred and twenty days. A stream of dirt falls from his fist onto his shadow. The shadow is not his. It has the shape of a conquering warrior in plates of armor and a pointed helm. The warrior writhes but the bonds of holy earth hold him fast. He tries to draw his sword but he cannot.

The wind rises. I raise an arm to protect myself and turn. The old man and the plane tree are gone. In place of them sits Mullah. He is unchanged from the days of my boy-hood, except that where the soldiers cut off his beard, it has grown back in strands of shining white light. His hand is outstretched and our village dogs are coming to sniff it, expecting treats. I go towards Mullah but he looks up and gives me this sad smile, pointing me elsewhere. I follow his hand, and walk over to Sher Khan.

I cannot see his face, it is wreathed in a cool and peace-ful flame. But there is no mistaking him. Blood gleams at his neck and shoulders and waist, all the places where the King's men cut off his limbs, so that each corner of the realm might have its own piece and look upon the wages of rebellion. Yet the wounds are stuffed with grass to staunch the bleeding, and he is moving smoothly enough. There is no sword, no bow, no gun in sight. He is as he loved to be. One moment he cuts a shank of meat, tossing pieces into an iron pot. In the next, he takes up an awl to mend someone else's sandals.

A hand grabs me and spins me around. I find myself looking at one of the King's soldiers, face shadowed by turban and helm. The soldier shoves a stone into my chained hands. When I look up, the blessed dead are lined up before me. This is what the soldiers did, to pass the long summer days. None of us ever knew who would be chosen for a stoning, who would be forced to cast the stones.

The soldier raises his fist. I shy from it, and sob, and throw. Even before the stone strikes home, they push another into my hand.

Again and again I throw, stoning Sher Khan and Mullah and the rest of the saints. As I do so, I see the ghosts all around me, soldiers and rebels, playing out the same story in different ages. There are those who have come before me, and those who will come after. The King's soldiers shove us and hoot. And we throw. And we throw.

"I am there," I said. "I will always be there. I survived the prison, meaning my hand held the stones. I murdered my friends and my comrades. I dishonored their bodies and their dreams. And I lived, but what could living ever mean after that? That's how you found me, drifting in the wind."

"You are saying," Mina said slowly, "we deserve each other because we are both monsters."

"I am saying," I replied, "that we are more than our crimes. That apart, each of us was struggling through our own river of blood. But together, we slew a monster."

Mina closed her eyes and exhaled softly. "I thought slaying a monster would be enough. I thought about turning around many times on the road here. He's gone now, and we don't have to run anymore. We could even go back to our people in the highlands. But they gave me over to a monster, Sado, and you fought at my side to bring him down. There's nobody left here for me but you."

The waves brushed the shore below, and a fantasy of the future brushed across me. I could see Mina and I in familiar alleys and familiar markets, walking under terraces and awnings we recognized, hearing the chatter of languages and peoples we understood. What we knew might bring comfort for a time. But there was only one true solace for me, and I knew where it was.

"I am still at your side," I said.

"But to what end?" she asked.

"To whatever end," I replied.

"What if I told you I've spoken to the fishermen?" she said. "That some of them row passengers down the coast, to a port town from where the dhows and sambuks sail out all the way out to the land of the Arabs, and the southern isles beyond? What if I told you I want to get on one of those boats and maybe never come back?"

"To whatever end," I repeated.

"And if I brought you all this way, even so wounded," she said, "simply because I wanted you with me?"

"Do you know how I would feel if you hadn't?" I said.

Mina paused. "Yes. I think I do."

"Together, then," I said.

"To whatever end?" Mina said.

I squeezed her hand in the dovecote's shadow. "To whatever end."

There was dusk caught in Mina's eyes. A few stray locks curled down to the corner of her mouth. The tattoo at the corner of her eye was almost hidden. The evening was closing in around us, but there was light enough left for me to see her smile.

It was in that hour that we came down to the sea, the three of us, Mina's arm steadying me, Khosh Qadam limping at our side: that same evening hour in which we had first seen one another weeks ago, the hour when the starlight falls across the earth, and the night sweeps the mountains away, and all the strays gather in the streets of towns and villages alike. A cool breeze snatched at my body and tugged at my spirit, and I held her on the gloomy paths leading to our fate. Together we moved along those paths, stepping from a shore without ocean to an ocean without shore, and all that would ever matter again was that she was there, closer to me than my own shadow, closer than my jugular vein.

Translations

Epigraph

Water cannot be sundered by the blows of a club.
Anonymous

Chapter One

My whole life has flown by with this one desire
That you might ask me, "Who are you, who might you be?"
Rahman

Chapter Two

Sunlight never finds its way into a roofed chamber
Better that the heart be rent and torn by some grief
Hamid

Chapter Three

Lost in my fancies, I took myself to be a king
When I woke, I found myself an ash-stained dervish
Anonymous

Chapter Four

Go, my love, God be your friend
My tattoos and curls shall keep you
Anonymous

Chapter Five

Come Hallaj's fate of gibbet and flung stones
Never shall I repent of your love
Hamid

Chapter Six

Delay the call for prayer, talib
I've only just reached my lover's arms
Anonymous

Chapter Seven

The time shall come, my love
For us to pick up our guns and go, hand in hand, to war
Anonymous

Chapter Eight

And we are closer to him than his jugular vein.
Quran

Acknowledgements

To the zayirs, sharing stories under the chinars on slow summer afternoons. To the khosh nawisan and their evening hospitality. To the ghosts and the strays.

To Rahman, Hamid, Bedil, Hallaj, Mutanabbi, Ibn Arabi, and the anonymous lyricists whose words flow through the warp and weft of this story. To my aunts, whose own stories are the tree from which my tales branch out. To my grandfathers, who wove literature into lives that keep lighting the way for mine.

To the teachers who lettered me, all those who breathed encouragement and wonder into my days. To Shahzad Bashir most especially, the monsoon on the desert. To my family in Miami, who welcomed me into the orchard of the Borras clan.

To my editor and publisher, Jennifer Crispin. You took a chance on my story, cut into its narrative bones, coaxed wonders from the openings. To Guoldu, who stitched perfect art for this tale. To Maria Haskins and Bogi Takács, for giving generously of your time and thought. To the fabulous editors I have been fortunate to meet in the market of narrative. To you, dear reader, for having passed some time here with me.

To all my friends across the years and the seas. As I worked the matter of this story, I drew sustenance from the free republic of Ali Karamustafa, Ali Karjoo-Ravary, CJ Uy, Hadel Jarada, Jenna Hanchey, Matt Bell, Pasoun Nasseri, and Saleh Al-Kharboosh. To my first readers, dear brothers, whose eyes sharpened both the story and my renderings of its verses: to Will Sherman, the sound of meaning's lute playing riot. To Sabauon Nasseri, my flesh and my nails.

To my mother and father, my light ubiquitous, cast without any lamp and coursing forever through my days. My mother's voice is the wing by which my soul soars. When I look at my father, I see the grandest of mountains.

For Caro: you are the very beating of my heart. As I move on the page and off of it, it is to you, for you, with you.

Istanbul, 17 December 2025

Tanvir Ahmed is a storyteller and historian. His short fiction has appeared in various magazines and collections, including *The Year's Best Fantasy* and *The Horror Library*. He earned his doctorate from Brown University writing on medieval Islamic history, was once a competitive fencer, and is an avid boxer. He lives in the American Southwest.

Dancing Star
Press

Dancing Star Press is an independent publisher based in Lansing, Michigan. Our mission is to publish speculative fiction that shows that not only can monsters be defeated, but so can oppressive governments and other forms of social control. We believe in finding hope in the apocalypse, joy in a dystopia, and people and peoples finding their power.

Check out our other titles and leave a comment or review on your favorite social media platform.

www.ingramcontent.com/pod-product-compliance
Lightning Source LLC
Chambersburg PA
CBHW061455210726

48287CB00007B/2526